ISTANBUL
EXPRESS

T. DAVIS BUNN

ISTANBUL EXPRESS

BETHANY HOUSE PUBLISHERS
MINNEAPOLIS, MINNESOTA 55438

Istanbul Express
Copyright © 1995
T. Davis Bunn

This story is entirely a creation of the author's imagination.
No parallel between any persons, living or dead, is
intended.

Cover illustration by Joe Nordstrom

Published by Bethany House Publishers
A Ministry of Bethany Fellowship, Inc.
11300 Hampshire Avenue South
Minneapolis, Minnesota 55438

Printed in the United States of America.

Library of Congress Cataloging-in-Publication Data

CIP applied for

ISBN 1–55661–383–0   CIP

TO AL AND EVAN STUART

With heartfelt thanks for
all that you have taught,
all that you have shared,
all that you are.

Books by T. Davis Bunn

The Quilt
The Gift
The Messenger

The Maestro
The Presence
Promises to Keep
Riders of the Pale Horse

The Priceless Collection
Secret Treasures of Eastern Europe

1. *Florian's Gate*
2. *The Amber Room*
3. *Winter Palace*

Rendezvous With Destiny

1. *Rhineland Inheritance*
2. *Gibraltar Passage*
3. *Sahara Crosswind*
4. *Berlin Encounter*
5. *Istanbul Express*

T. DAVIS BUNN, originally of North Carolina, spent many years in Europe as an international business executive. Fluent in several languages, his successful career took him to over 40 countries of the world. But in recent years his faith and his love of writing have come together for a new direction in his life. This extraordinarily gifted novelist is able to craft high-powered political and historical fiction, as well as simple yet compelling stories like *The Quilt* and *The Gift*. Davis's aim is to entertain and inspire. He and his wife, Isabella, currently make their home in Henley-on-Thames, England.

Chapter One

By the fourth day, the glamour and the romance were wearing awfully thin.

Despite the wear and tear of war, the Orient Express remained a luxurious way to grow bored. The lounge and dining compartments were resplendent with leather, brass, and oil-stained wood. Jake and Sally's compartment offered fold-up beds, an accordion-style writing desk, high-back leather seats, and embroidered footrests. There were bells to call the waiter, wine steward, and porter. The nightstand was a model of rolling ingenuity, with the little crystal water goblet nestled in a suede-lined brass well, the pen with its capped inkwell and writing pad, and the locket-sized brass chest for chocolates—heaven forbid that they should wake up in the middle of the night faint with hunger. The daintily appointed bathroom had brought a squeal of delight from Sally. It reminded Jake of one of those expensive dollhouses, perfect to look at, and impossibly uncomfortable for anyone over nine inches tall.

Sally baffled him utterly. Since they had boarded the train in Paris, his normally sensible wife had stayed happily entertained on nothing. Whenever his pacing brought him within reach, she bestowed a delighted smile, then went back to her book or her perusal of the window or her happy chatter with another passenger. No matter that the passenger was about as interesting as a large rock and had the intellectual depth of a sparrow. No matter that the train was now more than two and a half days behind schedule. No matter that there was not a single book in the train's meager library with all its pages intact, or that it had rained continually since their departure.

Nor did it appear to matter that their best friends and companions for the trip had effectively abandoned them. The honeymooning couple, Jasmyn and Pierre, had emerged from their compartment only six times in four days, and in that period had spoken a grand total of nine words to anyone else. Nine. Jake had been counting. He had nothing else to do.

Their stop in Zagreb the morning of the fourth day was another excuse for more baffling enthusiasm from Sally. She rushed to him, grabbed his hand, pulled him out on the platform. "Look over there, do you see that woman?"

"Barely," he grunted, shielding his eyes from rain whipped sideways by the wind. "You really find this interesting?"

"Are you kidding? She's great. They're all great. It's like traveling inside a Victorian novel. The dowager empress, the English governess, the mysterious millionaire." She hugged Jake with excitement. "I never thought I would be doing anything quite like this."

"Me neither." Jake released a pent-up sigh. "Or for so long."

"Oh, you." She released him. "I wish there were

some way I could make this last another couple of weeks."

Jake showed genuine alarm. "Don't even think about it."

She examined his face, then pulled him over so they were shielded by the train. "You're still worried about not having heard from Harry?"

"Among other things." Harry Grisholm was Jake's superior in his newfound field of international intelligence, and someone Jake admired tremendously. It was Harry who had followed Jake to Marseille and talked him into taking the Istanbul post. Harry was supposed to lead their project from the United States embassy in Ankara. After Jake had accepted the position, Harry had pressed upon them the urgency of the project, and stressed that there was not even time to return to England before beginning the new assignment. Every minute was required to bring Jake up to speed. Someone else would see to packing their belongings and shipping them to Turkey.

A scant three days later, with Jake's briefing barely started, Harry Grisholm had been called back to London. The command from headquarters had left the little man helplessly fuming. Furthermore, something in the tone of his orders had left him cautious about having Jake accompany him back. Instead, Harry had suggested they take a slower passage to Istanbul via the newly reopened Orient Express. Then he had departed, promising to make every possible haste to join them along the way and continue Jake's briefing.

Since then, there had been no sign of Harry, nor any word at all.

"He probably heard we were being delayed and

went on by air," Sally offered. "He'll be there when we arrive."

"And if he isn't?" Jake's worries congealed in his gut. "I'm supposed to have so much money arriving I won't count it, just stick it on the scale and round it up to the nearest pound. And all I've been told so far is that I'm supposed to make careful note of how it's being spent."

"He told you more than that," Sally chided.

"Not all that much." Glumly Jake watched the platform vendors shout their way along the train's length, selling everything from espresso to fur hats. "And not nearly enough to get the job done."

"Well, there's nothing you can do about it now." At the sound of the train's whistle, Sally tugged him back up the steps. "Now promise me you'll try to have a good time, okay? We'll get there soon enough."

The lounge would have been his perfect hideaway, had not every other man in the train decided the same thing. And Jake was the only one who did not smoke. The puff of choice was either a cigar that brought to mind the word *pumpernickel* or pipe tobacco that smelled of a long-dead cherry orchard.

There were three distinct groups of passengers. In the majority were the men who wore tuxedos with starched high collars and white bow ties—at eleven o'clock in the morning. They held themselves as aloof as possible while being crammed together for days on end. They traveled with two hard-edged intentions; to return to a life of ease, and to restore their sense of position and status. To their minds, the recent war was an inconvenience, now best forgotten.

Next came the wealthy European business owners, in bright suits and nervous manners. Many were war profiteers, who quaffed back bucket-sized goblets of brandy and scotch as they gambled recklessly, and talked in voices that would have made foghorns shrivel with envy.

A third group, far smaller than the others, were professional travelers. These bore the hard-earned stamp of distant gazes and guarded reserve. Jake would have liked to meet them, but they came and went like the wind, holding themselves utterly aloof from the others. Sally had managed to briefly meet two, an English governess traveling to Damascus to take up a position with a sheik's family, and a Belgian missionary returning to his flock and family in Beirut. Travel still suffered from war-inflicted wounds, and for the time being all safe roads ran through Istanbul. Thus the Orient Express, such as it was, remained the best overland passage to the mysterious east.

Except for Sally, there were no gawking tourists on the train; postwar rationing saw to that. As for Pierre and Jasmyn, Jake did not bother to count them at all. For all he saw of his friends, they might as well not have been on the train.

Under Harry Grisholm's persistent urgings, the time following Pierre and Jasmyn's wedding had passed in such feverish preparation that the new-lyweds had managed only a single day on a secluded Riviera estate. After a half-dozen urgent messages had brought the couple home early, Pierre had declared to Harry and everyone else within range that a one-day honeymoon was like being led to the wedding banquet and being granted a single bite of dry toast. Although clearly pleased to be assigned a post near his friend, Pierre had boarded the train intent upon making up for time lost.

The fifth morning dawned as gray and wet as the previous four. As was his habit, Jake rose at first light and made his way to the dining car. These solitary breakfasts were his only chance to be outside their compartment without being surrounded by smoke and noise. A sleepy waiter took his order and left him alone.

Sometime during the night, the train had pulled into yet another nameless Yugoslav village and stopped. Around the red-brick station spread a small hamlet of ancient cottages. The village was surrounded by fields of grain bowed under the weight of unending rain. Jake smiled his thanks when the waiter brought his coffee. He took a first sip, unbuttoned his shirt pocket, drew out his small New Testament, and was soon lost in his study.

"May I join you?"

Jake's head popped up. A rather sheepish Pierre stood waiting patiently beside his table. Jake motioned to the seat across from him. "By all means."

"What can you recommend?" The Frenchman slid into the leather-upholstered bench with a quiet sigh. "I regret to say that until now all my meals have been served in the compartment."

"I've noticed." His friend looked rested, but a little pale, and his voice sounded drained. "Everything is great."

"Then that is precisely what I shall have," Pierre said as the waiter approached. "A breakfast of everything."

"Very good, sir." The English waiter had the un-

shakable calm of one trained to handle the most difficult of passengers. "Eggs, bacon, sausage, tomato,
mushrooms, kippers, beans, and fried bread?"

"Nix on the beans and kippers," Jake advised.

"As my friend suggests. And extra on whatever else
you said," Pierre amended. "As well as a pot of that
coffee."

"Right you are, sir." The waiter turned and left.

Pierre turned his attention to the window. Outside,
a group of Slavic dancers entertained on the platform,
though it was doubtful how many of the passengers
were awake enough to enjoy the spectacle. Accordions
and fiddles flew through ancient mountain melodies as
the beribboned dancers gyrated and kicked their heels
to incredible heights. Security was ominous and everywhere. The official police wore belted woolen over-
coats with holstered pistols at their waists.

Pierre observed, "We are not moving."

"We've been doing a lot of that," Jake agreed.

Pierre rubbed the side of his face. "As I recall, we
were supposed to arrive in Istanbul the night before
last."

"Right again."

"Yet this does not look much like Istanbul to me."

"If it did," Jake replied, "then somebody's managed
to move the city about four hundred miles."

"Ah." Pierre examined the plate of scrambled eggs
and toast that the waiter set down in front of Jake.
"That does not look very substantial."

Jake discarded the first comment that came to mind
and made do with, "I don't have much appetite in the
morning."

Pierre turned to the waiter. "Your chef understands
that I wish to have a large portion of everything?"

"You will be digging for a week to find the plate, sir," the waiter replied calmly.

Pierre accepted the news with a grave nod. "That is what I like about the British," he said after the waiter had moved off. "They may mangle every other meal until you cannot tell whether you are dining on smoked salmon or roast beef, but their breakfasts almost make up for it."

"I think the food has been pretty good throughout the day," Jake replied.

"Then the day chef must be French." It was a statement of fact, not a proposition. Pierre turned back to the window. "Do you have any idea where we are?"

"Somewhere in Yugoslavia. The border guards came through, remember?"

"Ah, yes. Tito's new thugs." There was a brief furrowing of Pierre's expressive face, then, "That was yesterday, no?"

"That was two days ago," Jake replied gently.

"Of course. How time flies when you are standing still." A fleeting confusion swept across Pierre's mobile features. "Did not Harry Grisholm say that we were in a hurry?"

"Right again," Jake confirmed. "I guess it's the same as the army, hurry up and wait."

"Ah, here we are." Pierre's interest sparked as the waiter presented a plate arranged in neat layers. On the bottom was a liberal foundation of bacon, upon which nine or ten sausages had been set like pudgy logs. Surrounding these was an array of sliced tomatoes and wedges of fried bread. And laid gently on top was a blanket of six sunny-side-up eggs.

"Chef says that he will personally deliver seconds on anything," the waiter said, "free of charge."

"Please thank your maitre d'," Pierre replied solemnly. "I believe this shall do me quite well for the moment."

"If you eat all that," Jake declared, "we're going to carry you off this train feet first."

"If I eat all this," Pierre responded, grasping knife and fork with grim determination, "I shall hopefully survive the next four hundred miles."

"These delays are such a nuisance." The woman was dressed and coiffured from a bygone day, layer upon starchy neat layer, in a manner that told the world she traveled with a full-time maid. Her heavy jewels clinked and glistened with each grand movement. "I told the conductor again last night that I simply must get on to Istanbul. Do you know what he said? 'It is the war, madame.' As if the war hadn't been over for ages. I cannot imagine how one is expected to get on, what with the quality of service these days. If he had ever dared to offer my father such a quip, the man would have been sent packing in an instant, I can promise you that."

Sally hid her smile behind a discreet cough. For ten o'clock in the morning, her compartment was surprisingly crowded. Jasmyn sat beside her, her exotic features quietly radiant in the way of a happy bride, her dark eyes observing the scene from a contented distance. Across from Jasmyn, beside the rather obese English lady, sat the English governess, quiet and prim in her neat gray suit. Beside her sat a Swiss woman whom the governess had brought along; she had not spoken a word since her arrival.

Sally asked, "Do you have something urgent await-ing you in Istanbul?"

"Well, of course. You don't think I would make this beastly trip for my health?" Mrs. Fothering had the full-throated voice of a very large goose. "Phyllis Hol-lamby is having her annual gathering next Wednesday. You of course know Mrs. Hollamby."

"I'm afraid not," Sally replied.

"Oh, my dear, you simply must." As Mrs. Fothering played with the folds of her dress, her ring turned the rainy gray light into a cascading rainbow. The central diamond was as large as a robin's egg. "Why, Phyllis Hollamby is a pillar of Istanbul expatriate society."

Sally smiled and glanced contentedly around her cabin. The woodwork gleamed of oil and polish, the seats were heavy brocade with starched pillowcases over the headrests. When she and Jake were at dinner, the carriage butler arrived to fold down the beds, plump the eiderdown quilts, and set out a serving of hot chocolate. Sally found it all utterly delightful. "My husband and I are traveling there for the first time."

"Oh yes, I recall something now. An ambassadorial posting or some such, isn't that correct?"

She had to think a moment to recall the title Harry had discussed, the one intended to cover Jake's real purposes. "Jake has been appointed assistant consul."

"How perfectly fascinating, I'm sure." Mrs. Foth-ering gave the watch-pendant attached to her ample bosom a nearsighted inspection. "My goodness, just look at the time. I do hope my maid has managed to complete the pressing of my day dress. Well, if you will excuse me, I have a thousand things to see to. Good day, my dear. You must be sure and remember to look up Phyllis Hollamby."

"Cross my heart," Sally said, her smile breaking through.

Mrs. Fothering bestowed a ponderous nod upon the entire compartment. "Ladies."

As the compartment door slid shut behind her, the train's whistle gave a wheezing toot, the car jerked, and they began to move. The Swiss woman spoke for the first time. "Finally."

"It certainly is nice to be moving again," Sally agreed.

"I thought she would never stop," the governess told her acquaintance.

"Nor I." The Swiss woman was of late middle age and had the sun-dried complexion of someone who lived for the outdoors. Her clothes were expensive yet severe, and magnified the sharp lines of her chin and nose. Her eyes were gray and direct as they turned toward Sally. "My dear, your husband is in grave danger."

"What?" The word was a gasp torn from deep within her.

Instead of replying, the woman turned toward Jasmyn and continued, "Yours, too, I would assume, although his appointment came so swiftly it is hard to know who has been informed. Rest assured, however, that once his position is made clear, his life will also be in jeopardy."

"There is always danger," Jasmyn said, as tense and upright as Sally. "But Turkey is secure."

"I assure you it is not."

"Who are you?"

"That does not matter." She waited while the English governess rose and discreetly checked the hallway in both directions. "Listen, for that addle-headed woman has left us with little time. You are aware of the name Ataturk?"

"Of course," Sally replied, striving for calm, though it cost her dearly. Ataturk had led Turkey after World War One had ended the rule of the Ottoman caliphs. He had fought to draw Turkey closer to the West, and had severed ties with traditional allies and colonies in the Middle East and Africa. He had established alliances with Europe and America, granted women equal status as citizens for the first time in a modern Islamic state, and even changed the alphabet to Roman script. This much she had gained from the hurried tutoring given them prior to their departure.

"Ever since Ataturk's death, his followers have been attacked from all sides," the Swiss woman said. "Turkey's government is still openly sympathetic to the West, but its enemies are openly anti-Western. And the Communists are fomenting trouble wherever they can. They see your husband and the power he represents as a threat."

Sally glanced toward Jasmyn, saw that she was pale and tight-lipped. She placed one hand over the two clenched tightly in Jasmyn's lap and said as evenly as she could manage, "I asked who you were."

"You will be contacted upon your arrival," the woman replied, rising to her feet. "Someone will approach you and ask if you have happened to visit Topkapi, the sultans' summer palace. It was closed to visitors during the war and only reopened six months ago." She reached for the handle, halted. "This is most important. You must not forget the password."

"Topkapi, the sultans' summer palace," Sally repeated. "But how—"

"Do not try to contact either of us again. And be

careful what you decide to tell your husbands." She slid the door open and stepped outside. The governess followed her.

"Whatever happens, wherever you might be, as soon as you hear those words, stop and follow. Your very lives may depend upon this."

Chapter Two

That's all?" Jake looked from one woman to the other. "No idea of what we're heading toward?"

"Or whether we should go at all," Pierre added.

Sally examined the men's faces in turn. "Would you just get a load of you two."

Jasmyn clearly agreed. She rounded on her husband, said, "You don't have to appear so pleased."

Pierre's flexible features tried hard for wide-eyed innocence. "I am simply eager to arrive at the bottom of this, ma cherie."

But Jasmyn was not so easily convinced. She crossed her arms, huffed, "It is as though you are happy to see our honeymoon interrupted."

"Perish the thought," Pierre said, then made the mistake of glancing at his watch. "Although it has been quite a bit longer—"

"It seems like if those women were going to go to all the trouble of contacting us," Jake amended hastily, "they would have had some distinct purpose in mind." He found himself not minding the news at all, or the new tone to the voyage. But he did not like having Sally read him so easily.

"Something more definite than just passing on a

general warning," Pierre agreed. "We already know the situation is dangerous."

Sally rounded on Jake. "Since when did you know?"

Jasmyn showed alarm. "Why was I not informed?"

"Nobody has said anything definite," Jake said soothingly. "But Stalin is dangerous, and it just stands to reason that any post this close to the bear's lair would have some risk attached."

Sally returned to perusing the gray scene outside her window. The rain had finally stopped, but no break had appeared in the heavy, brooding clouds. The train wound its way along a craggy hillside, the sense of speed increased by grinding wheels and shuddering cabins. No amount of plush comfort could disguise the fact that the track was in a dismal state of repair.

"I don't like it," she said finally.

"Well, what do you want us to do?" Jake grasped her hand, found the fingers cold as ice. "Turn around?"

"I want you to be careful," she said quietly.

"I always am. You know that."

"More than that," she said, turning back around, her features creased with worry. "I want you to survive."

They crossed the Bulgarian border late in the night, the passage signaled by squealing brakes and heavy boots and rough-hewn voices. It seemed to Sally that all the world was asleep except for her. Above her head, Jake turned over, the bunk creaking softly at his movement. Her head rang with the words of warning spoken that morning, words that had transformed their train journey from an adventure to a prison.

The compartment door slid partway open, the curtains chinking gently to permit both light and a hulking form. She fended sleep as a flashlight scampered about the room, resting briefly upon her, then moving on. She cracked one eyelid, caught a fleeting image of a peaked cap, badge, broad shoulders, narrowed eyes. Then the curtain dropped, the door slid shut, and they were alone.

Instantly a shudder of fear ran through her, a fear not of unknown guards, but of being trapped. Nowhere to run, no way to protect what was most important to her.

There was the sound of movement, soft as a cat, as Jake slipped from his bunk and crouched down beside her. Strong arms enveloped her, drawing her up and close and safe. She yielded to his strength and to her fears. "Oh, Jake."

"Shhh. I know." He slid into the bunk alongside her, never letting go of her for a moment. Giving her the comfort she craved. "It's going to be all right."

"How do you know?" Worries scampered about her mind. "What if—"

"Not now," he murmured, nestling into the space where shoulder joined neck. He took a long breath, something he often did when holding her like that, taking the scent of her down deep. The simple act consoled her far more than words. He was here and he was with her. He murmured, "Where is the strong and independent Sally I married?"

"She got left behind in Marseille," she said, trying for humor, but the smile beyond her grasp. "Sorry."

"Think we should go back for her?"

There it was, the invitation she had been hoping for,

yearning to hear, the chance to turn around and leave behind all that had entered her life with the pair of women and their obscure message. But she felt Jake's arms about her, this man she loved with all her heart, a man who lived for life on the edge. "No," she sighed. "I guess not."

"That's my girl," he said, holding her tight, giving with his embrace what words could not, remaining there and close until sleep drew up and carried her away.

The train screeched around a sharp bend, and Sally awoke to another rainy morning. Jake was still there, one arm under his head and the other draped across her, the two of them somehow comfortable and cozy in the tiny bunk. She dimly recalled being awakened briefly around dawn, as the train rumbled into a station with squealing brakes and chuffing steam. There had been the sound of voices outside the window, strange after so much isolation, and she had lifted the edge of the window shade far enough to read the station sign overhead—Sofia. A shadow had flitted past her window, and she had let the shade drop back into place. Before long, the safety and comfort of Jake's slumbering closeness had drawn her back into sleep.

Jake stirred, on the edge of wakefulness. His arm tightened, searched, recalled the feel of her, all without reaching the shore of consciousness. She buried her nose into his hair, softly kissed his ear. He responded with a half-murmur. As smoothly as she could, she drew her arm up and around his neck, reveling in his strength and warmth. She nestled in, surrounded by her man, safe and isolated even here.

"Night before last I decided I would never be comfortable on this train," Jake said sleepily. "And that was trying to fit into my bunk all by my lonesome."

She raised up enough to watch his sleepy eyes open, the little boy there with the man. Such a wondrous moment of intimacy, each one the very first time. "And now look at you."

"I know what it is," he said. "This bunk is bigger. You've been keeping it a secret."

She kissed him softly. "Good morning, my hero."

His eyes softened, the light strengthened. "It really is you, isn't it?"

She nodded. "Right where I belong."

His arms tightened around her. "How did I ever come to deserve this?"

Suddenly the power of her love threatened to expand farther than her chest was able to hold. Breath came in a little catch, forcing itself about her swollen heart, the pressure pushing tears about her eyes. "Don't you ever change, Jake Burnes," she whispered, her arms holding him as close as she could possibly manage. "Not ever."

Beyond Sofia their world suddenly altered. Scarcely had they entered the dining car, seated themselves across from Pierre and Jasmyn, and exchanged smiles and comments about couples who did not eat breakfast until almost noon than the sun emerged. The sight was so startling and so wondrous after five days of unending gray that the entire car, waiters included, broke into a cheer.

Under the fresh sunlight, the train gleamed with seedy grandeur. The war years had left no funds for new paint, yet the ancient blue cars gleamed with recent polish. Not even eight hundred miles of hard travel could disguise the glorious bronzework.

Outside their window, the countryside was undergoing a drastic change. The clearing sky looked down upon a landscape that was more accustomed to heat and dust than cold and rain. Rocky clefts proved stubborn homes for gnarled pines and scraggly undergrowth. Hillsides grew steeper, the contrasts between green and rock starker. Goats and sheep bleated as they scampered in search of meager fodder, followed by young boys who whistled and waved as the train swept by.

"Colonel Burnes, I presume?"

Jake turned from the window, looked up at the urbane gentleman with his steady gaze. "Yes?"

The man clicked his heels and gave a stiff minuscule bow. "Dimitri Kolonov, at your service." He turned to the others and gave a lofty smile. "And this must be Major Pierre Servais, and these beautiful ladies Mrs. Servais and Mrs. Burnes. A great honor, I assure you."

"Forgive me, m'sieur," Pierre said, collecting himself first. "I do not recall hearing of you."

"Of course not." The man himself was in direct opposition to his dress and his manner. He had the hard-boiled look of a veteran fighter. His lips were two bloodless lines, his teeth sheered as though worn by years of clenched jaws. His eyes were as lifeless as marbles. Kolonov reached for his breast pocket and removed a slender yellow envelope. "Perhaps this will help clarify matters."

Jake accepted the flimsy envelope, read the words "Western Union" and then something beneath in Cyrillic. Instead of opening the envelope, Jake asked, "Are you Russian?"

"I do indeed have that honor." Kolonov motioned to the empty table across the narrow aisle from their own. "May I?"

"I do not recall seeing you on the train before," Pierre said.

"That is natural, as I only came aboard in Sofia," Kolonov replied, taking Pierre's remark as an invitation and seating himself. "Like yourselves, I have been pulled away from other duties at short notice."

Jake opened the envelope, noticed the last word. "It's from Harry," he told his companions. Jake read the telegram first silently, then again aloud:

HAVE BEEN UNAVOIDABLY DETAINED IN LONDON. YOU ARE TO PROCEED TO ISTAN-BUL AND COMMENCE DUTIES WITHOUT ME. BEARER OF THIS MESSAGE IS DIMITRI KO-LONOV FORMERLY OF NKVD AND NOW SEC-ONDED TO SOVIET CONSULATE IN ISTAN-BUL. I ASSURE YOU THAT YOU MAY TRUST HIM FULLY AND REMIND YOU OF ASSIS-TANCE GIVEN BY MR RASULI. REGARDS HARRY.

"I do hope this has explained the situation," Ko-lonov said.

"No doubt," Pierre murmured, his voice a quiet purr. "May I trouble you for the telegram, Jake?"

Jake handed over the yellow sheet, caught sight of a courtier's smile creasing Pierre's otherwise blank face. He turned back to Kolonov, willing himself to remain as composed as his friend, acutely aware of the telegram's double message. Sultan Al-Rasuli, as Harry Grisholm well knew, ruled a fiefdom in Morocco's central highlands. He had held Pierre's brother, a former leader of the French Resistance, in his dungeons while offering to supply Patrique's head to the highest bidder.

"I don't see how much use I'm going to be to anyone," Jake said carefully to Kolonov. "Not only do I not have any training in diplomatic operations, but I'm not even fully briefed."

"Our departure was very hasty," Pierre added, maintaining his calm composure.

"Harry said it was imperative to get us into place," Jake finished. "He insisted that our training could be completed once we were settled. All I know is that the first batch of building funds were to arrive three weeks ago, and that someone needed to be in position to manage their dispersal."

That much had been clear from the news and from Harry's hasty summary. Relief funds had been pouring into Europe since the war, including some construction funds for Turkey. Not much, compared to what was being poured into Germany and Italy and France, but what was relatively small by international standards was a staggering amount in Jake's eyes.

"Then what happens, but you have been trapped upon this train for five days now," the Russian commiserated, oozing slick sympathy. "Never fear, my new friends. I have it on strictest record that we shall experience no further delays and shall arrive in Istanbul by daybreak tomorrow." He flashed another humorless smile. "I have personally spoken with the man at the controls, and assured him that otherwise the train will be forced to find itself another engineer."

All four joined him in a moment's tense laughter, and shared blank looks about their table. Jake then said, "NKVD. That's the initials of the Soviet secret service, am I right?"

"It has indeed been my honor to serve my country as you have served yours," Kolonov announced proudly. "Which shall grant us wonderful opportunities to exchange our stories and know-how, did I say that correctly, know-how?"

"Absolutely," Jake said.

"Your English is impeccable," Sally assured him, her tone as cool as her gaze.

"Thank you, Mrs. Burnes. And speaking as one professional to another, Colonel, I must tell you, your lack of training matters not a bit. Why, I myself have not the first iota of experience in such matters as the distribution of funds. And just look at yourselves. What in your military backgrounds has prepared you to handle so much money?"

"Not a lot."

"Precisely!" Kolonov thumped his open palm triumphantly upon the table. "So why have we been selected for these positions?"

"Search me."

"As figureheads!" Kolonov beamed at all and sundry. "We shall be paraded here and there, attend the openings and meet the government leaders, be seen at all the best functions. And why not, I ask you? We have served our countries through the hard times. Let the pencil pushers count the zeros and keep their books, that is what assistants are for. Is it not time that we should savor a little of the easy life?"

Before Jake could think up a response, Kolonov

gave a quick glance up and down the almost-empty car, then leaned conspiratorially across the aisle. "Listen, my friend, I tell you, this posting will do wonders for our careers. Just think of the contacts we shall make. And the businesses eager to win the contracts, why, two years of being wined and dined, then—"

"Oh, the honeymooning couple, how absolutely charming."

The overstuffed English woman, Mrs. Fothering, bustled over to loom above their table. "I was so looking forward to meeting the dashing French officer. And you must be the famous Colonel Burnes."

Jake caught Sally's silent flash of humor as he rose to his feet. "I don't know about the famous part, but the rest is right."

"Oh, stuff and nonsense. Medals were made to be worn, not hidden in a drawer, that's my motto."

"Jake, this is Mrs. Fothering." Sally's voice had the lilting charm of a carefully disguised smile. "She's traveling to Istanbul for a party to be given by Phyllis Hollamby."

"I don't know why I am surprised to find you were paying attention, my dear. You most certainly have the marks of a proper upbringing about you." She offered Jake a yellow claw of a hand, surprisingly parched and narrow given the ample size of the rest of her. "How do you do."

"Charmed, I'm sure." Jake motioned to where Pierre stood. "This is Major Pierre Servais and his wife, Jasmyn."

"Yes, I have already had the pleasure of meeting the lovely young bride." She extended her hand once more, gave a subdued cluck of pleasure when Pierre leaned over and kissed the air above her wrist, then purred, "Major."

"Won't you join us?" Jake asked, with all the sincerity he could muster, both because of Sally's sudden smile and because the Russian was clearly irritated by the interruption. Jake motioned toward him, said, "May I present Mr. Dimitri Kolonov, who has just joined the train in Sofia."

"How positively fascinating," she sniffed, and managed to avoid offering her hand by stumbling slightly as Jake held the back of her chair. "Oh, thank you—these blasted rails, they really should do something to smooth out this journey, don't you agree?"

"There has been a war on," Dimitri offered, resuming his seat.

"Just what the conductor told me," she said, her tone icy. "You and he must have a chat, I am sure you shall no doubt find positively hordes of things to discuss." She dredged up a smile for Pierre and Jasmyn and said, "Now then. You must tell me all about your ceremony. I positively adore weddings, particularly my own."

Pierre asked, "You are married?"

"Oh, my goodness, yes. Let me see now, is it three or four times? I never can remember. No, five, if you count the disastrous second try Alistair and I made. That was an utter mistake, I am sorry to say. But a positively beautiful wedding. Absolutely gorgeous. I had to forgive him for pressing me into giving it that second go since he let me fulfill my every wish with the wedding."

Kolonov rose to his feet, steadied himself as the train gave a squealing lurch, then bowed and said stiffly, "Perhaps we can speak further at another time."

"That'd be just swell," Jake said smoothly.

When the Russian had given the ladies a stiff bow and departed, Mrs. Fothering sniffed once more. "What an utterly beastly man. However did you meet him?"

"He met us," Pierre replied.

"Yes, that is the problem with his sort, I'm afraid." She rose to her feet, drawing them with her. "Well, I shan't keep you any longer."

"Oh, you mustn't rush off," Sally said.

Jake found himself liking the old dame, if for no other reason than that she had saved them from further time with the Russian. "Maybe you'd like to join us for dinner tonight?"

"What a positively gallant invitation. Alas, as I wish to be fresh for our arrival tomorrow, I shall most likely dine in my compartment." She reached across the table to take Sally's hand. "You must remember to look up Phyllis Hollamby when you arrive, my dear. And be sure to suggest that she show you Topkapi. No one knows the sultans' summer palace better than she."

Chapter Three

They entered Istanbul at the breathless hush of first light. The train wound past a series of dry-scrabble rises, farmland, and individual houses gradually giving way to dusty streets and ancient tenements. The buildings grew in size, the space between them lessened. Then they rounded the final rise, and before them stretched the glittering waters of the Bosphorus.

"This is perfect!" Sally flung her arms around Jake's neck and planted a kiss with perfect accuracy. "How ever did you arrange it all?"

Pierre covered his laughter with a discreet cough. Jasmyn rewarded them with a warm smile. Jake looked from one woman to the other and saw no trace of worry, nothing but the excitement of new beginnings. "What has come over you two?"

Jasmyn asked, "You are complaining?"

"Not at all."

"You just have us wondering," Pierre allowed, "after the long faces and worried voices of yesterday."

"Oh, hush, you two, and let's enjoy this." Sally's face was pushed up close to the glass. Without turning away she found Jake's hand and drew it into her lap.

"This is the first glimpse of our new home. Aren't you the least little bit excited?"

"Absolutely," Jake agreed, then nodded to Pierre's shrug. Women.

The sun rose huge and smoldering into an empty sky. The light turned the entire world a ruddy orange. Cargo ships plied the fiery waters like vessels of old, their scarred and battered hulks transformed into ships of mirrored gold. Tiny fishing craft spun and darted about the behemoths, glittering fairy boats whose nets rose and fell like gossamer wings.

They followed a gradual curve around the water's edge. Then they ducked inland and were swallowed by the tall buildings of a great metropolis. Only this particular city was dotted with structures beyond time—crumbling aqueducts, remains of medieval walls, a city garden sprouting a forest of Roman columns. Everywhere rose the slender needles of minarets, the mosque towers from which the Muslim faithful were called to prayer.

Jake waited until Sally turned her beaming face back to the cabin to ask, "What's with the change this morning?"

"Oh, you," she smiled. "Isn't it enough just to sit here and be excited about everything that's up ahead?"

"You've been acting strange since yesterday," Jake persisted. "One minute you're as worried as I've ever seen, the next and you're like a little kid at Christmas."

"Not just Sally," Pierre added, watching his new wife.

"It's out in the open now," Sally said, refusing to release her excitement, her eyes stealing more glances out the window as the train wound through the slowly awakening city.

"What, the Russian?"

"He was a snake," Jasmyn said definitely. "But at least we can now see who it is we face."

"Dimitri Kolonov is supposed to be an ally," Pierre reminded them.

Sally joined Jasmyn in a double-barrelled glare. Pierre raised hands in mock defeat. "I just thought somebody should mention it."

"He is a snake," Jasmyn repeated. "But a visible one."

"It wasn't the threat that scared me so," Sally said, facing Jake. "It was the fact that I was hit when I felt protected."

"And from such an unexpected direction," Jasmyn added.

"Seeing that these are real people brings everything back into focus," Sally went on. "It shrinks the danger down to size."

"There are a lot of risks here besides Kolonov," Jake reminded her quietly.

"Of course there are." Her dimpled smile returned. "You wouldn't want it any other way, neither of you would. And you both know it."

"My friend," Pierre offered, "I think we should accept that we are surrounded by superior minds."

The train chose that moment to slide into dusty shadows and enter the station. The engine chuffed in noisy relief, the whistle gave a long satisfied toot, the brakes squealed tiredly, and the train shuddered to a halt.

The little group remained seated, looking from one to another, until Pierre said, "Something is missing here."

"We need to start this adventure off right," Sally

agreed, reaching for Jasmyn's hand. "Jake, will you lead us in prayer?"

"Excellent, excellent. You arrived safe and sound." Dimitri Kolonov stepped up as they were unloading their bags, as cold and polished as an ice sculpture. "You do not have someone from your consulate here to help you with your cases? What a disgrace."

Jake accepted the larger satchel from Sally. "We're used to getting our hands dirty."

"Ah, but those days are behind you, Colonel," Kolonov responded, waving one gray-gloved finger. "Remember, that is what underlings are for, *nyet*?"

"Are you traveling with your wife and children, Mr. Kolonov?" Sally asked.

"Call me Dimitri, please. After all, we shall be seeing so much of each other."

"I can hardly wait," she said, smiling her thanks as Jake offered her a hand down from the train.

"Alas, my wife is unable to join me just yet." Kolonov gave a mock sigh. "The price one pays for an overseas assignment can be high."

"Colonel Burnes? Colonel Jake Burnes?"

Jake turned and called, "Over here."

A lean, sunburned young man hustled over. He started to salute, then realized he was in civilian clothes and forced his hand back down. "I'm Corporal Bailey, sir. The consulate sent me over to fetch you."

"You see, what did I tell you, my friends? A new life!" Kolonov beamed triumphantly. "Well, I simply must dash. You will all come and be my guests for dinner at the Soviet consulate, yes?"

"Soon as we're settled," Jake assured him, accepting the hand, then turning back to the young man. "This is my wife, Corporal."

"Ma'am." The young man waited impatiently for the Russian to shake Pierre's hand and bow a final time to the ladies before departing. His tone was insistent as he said, "We need to be shoving off, sir."

"Lead on, Corporal."

"Yessir. Is this, I mean, are you Major Servais?"

"I am."

"I have a message for you too, sir. The French consulate called to say you should check in immediately. I can drop you off, if you like. Then I'll take your wives and the gear over to your hotel." Not waiting for a response, he hefted as many valises as he could manage, and started for the exit.

Jake caught up with him. "What's the rush?"

"The whole consulate's all sixes and sevens, sir. You were supposed to get in a couple of days ago."

"Our train was delayed," Sally pointed out.

"I know, I mean, yes, ma'am. There's been radio traffic like you wouldn't believe about that as well."

Jake demanded, "As well as what?"

"I'm not supposed to say, sir," the corporal responded carefully. "My orders are to get you back to the consulate and do it on the bounce."

Scarcely had they all settled into the big consular sedan than the swarthy Turkish driver let in the clutch and squealed away. Jake leaned forward from his station in the backseat and demanded, "Why can't you tell me anything?"

"Leave him alone, Jake," Sally said quietly, her gaze on the scene zipping by outside their window. "He's just following orders."

The corporal shot her a grateful glance, then returned his attention to the front windshield in time to call, "Heads up," and grab for the top deck. The driver swung wide around an overloaded donkey cart, then swept back in front of the animal's nose and ducked down an alley.

Corporal Bailey turned around and said apologetically, "I'd yell at him, sir, but it wouldn't do any good."

Pierre nodded approvingly in the driver's direction, then announced brightly, "I do believe I am going to like it here."

The driver traveled with equal pressure on the gas pedal and the horn. The only one who seemed perturbed by their lightning dash through gradually thickening traffic was Jake. After they had come within a hairsbreadth of derailing a streetcar, Jake asked Jasmyn, "This doesn't bother you?"

"I was raised in Marseille," she reminded him.

"The French only wish they could drive like this," Pierre said in admiration. He turned to the corporal. "Where can I buy myself a car?"

"Here we are, sir," the corporal announced as the car swung through great iron gates and halted in a cobblestone courtyard. "I'll let them know the colonel's arrived, then be back to escort everyone else onward."

Jake slid from the car and turned a worried frown toward Sally, but she stopped him with a smile. "We'll be fine. You go see to business."

He followed the corporal across the plaza, taking in the central fountain and the porticoes and the sculpted trellises around tall upper-floor windows. "This is nice."

"It used to be some sultan's palace," the corporal

said, bouncing up grand front steps to hold the door for Jake. "There's a lot of them around here."

The entrance hall was grand in a seedy and ancient fashion. The ceiling curved up a full two stories, and the ancient marble-tiled floor was ribbed where eons of feet had trod shallow channels. Just inside the second set of double doors stood a waist-high desk and behind it a uniformed Marine. Corporal Bailey announced, "This is the colonel."

"Thank the heavens above," the second young man announced. "I mean, welcome to Istanbul, sir. I'll just go and tell the chief you're here."

The young man trotted down the long formal hall, then took the sweeping staircase three steps at a time. Jake turned to the corporal and asked, "The chief?"

"Meester Jake!" The delighted cry turned them back around as a corpulent little man came rushing down the stairs. "Eeet ees so excellent to have you arrive, oh my, yes, so very excellent!"

"I'll just go and see to your wife and the major." The corporal began another salute, then stopped himself, started to offer his hand, decided that was too informal, finally settled on, "Good luck, sir."

Jake watched the round little man come bouncing down the hall. Too much too fast. "This the chief?" he asked the corporal.

"Chief? What chief?" Stubby legs carried the little man up and in front of Jake. "I am Ahmet," he announced proudly, as though that were all the explanation anyone needed.

"He's building superintendent, but unofficially sort of chief dogsbody," Corporal Bailey explained, sidling for the door. "Whatever you need, he's the guy. Does some of the local hiring as well. Handles official red tape."

"Exactly, yes, is so!" Ahmet waved the corporal away without turning his dark eyes from Jake. "What you need, Ahmet finds. Even before you ask."

"Sounds like a quartermaster I once knew." Jake accepted the little man's hand, felt the damp fingers squeeze once and release.

Ahmet looked like a little balloon balanced on top of a bigger balloon, with almost no neck between head and body. A few remaining strands of hair had been allowed to grow long, then were greased and plastered in black pencil lines across his otherwise bald scalp. His mouth seemed permanently creased into a smile that did not reach his glittering black eyes.

"You will soon see, what Ahmet says is true." He waved his hand in the general direction of the consulate's interior. "I have office all ready, yes, with files and papers and desk and chair and even assistant."

Jake stared down at the little man. "You've hired personnel for me?"

"Mr. Burnes?" Jake turned to see a woman leading the uniformed Marine across the entrance chamber. "I am Mrs. Ecevit, assistant to the political officer. Welcome to Istanbul."

Jake straightened, forced down his ire at this Ahmet and the sensation of being railroaded. "Thank you."

"I hope you had a pleasant trip." The woman was as cool and official as her voice. Middle-aged, a strong face framed by dark hair disciplined into a tight bun. Dark suit, white shirt, no jewelry that he could see. Intelligent eyes. But distant. She gazed at him with calculating prudence.

"Not bad." Jake glanced back at Ahmet, saw he had frozen up in silent disapproval. The little man did not like Mrs. Ecevit, that much was clear. For this reason alone, Jake found himself drawn to the woman and her cold stare. "Sorry we were delayed."

"Yes, no one has been able to fathom why Mr. Grisholm suggested you travel by rail." Her words were overlaid with a slight accent, yet her English was precise as her manner. "Your late arrival has caused us all a tremendous amount of concern. Would you come with me, please?"

"Lead the way." He nodded in reply to the Marine's salute, followed her down the hall and up the carpeted stairs. Far overhead hung a chandelier of glittering crystal leaves. "This is some place."

"It belonged to the grand vizier of the last Ottoman sultan," she said, neither turning around nor taking any notice of her surroundings. "The Ataturk regime gave it to us as a consulate soon after the capital was moved to Ankara." She stopped before a great door whose frame was embellished with plaster carvings in an intricate Oriental design. She knocked, said to Jake, "In here, please."

"Mr. Burnes, thank goodness you've arrived." A gray-haired man ignored Jake's outstretched hand, grasped his upper arm, and guided him in. Jake twisted about to thank Mrs. Ecevit, but she was already closing the door. "I can't tell you what a crisis your delayed arrival has put us into."

"So everybody's been telling me."

"Take that seat, why don't you?" He directed Jake to the straight-backed chair placed front and center before his oversized desk. As an afterthought, he leaned across the desk and offered his hand. "Charles Fernwhistle, Consul General Knowles's Deputy Chief of Mission."

The man's handshake brought to mind a wet mop left overnight in a refrigerator. Jake made no move to sit. "Consul General who?"

"Knowles. Ah. You were expecting Gramble, I see. No, unfortunately he was recalled." Fernwhistle had the elongated neck of a crane, a bowtie, and a nervous manner. Each sentence was punctuated by a quick little tug of his tie, an adjustment of his glasses, a smoothing of his jacket. "A dispute with our Russian allies. Quite sudden."

Jake felt his sense of isolation growing. He remained standing. "The Russians are dictating the choice of our consul general?"

"Our *allies* have every right to request such changes, especially in such times of delicate negotiations. I happened to have served with Consul General Knowles in Mexico during the war."

"Mexico," Jake echoed.

"He was not consul general then, of course. Actually he held my position. Gramble, on the other hand, was, well, a military man, no real experience with this type of work. Still, it was quite a jolt to everyone when he was abruptly replaced."

"Yeah, you look all broken up over it," Jake remarked.

The nose tilted up one notch further. "Sit down, won't you." When Jake had eased himself into the seat, Fernwhistle said, "While military experience no doubt has its merits, unfortunately delicate negotiations require someone with a little more, well . . ."

Ability to cringe, Jake offered silently, and changed

the subject with, "So I guess it's up to you to tell me what's going on."

"There is unfortunately no time for that." A glimmer of satisfaction surfaced in Fernwhistle's bland voice. "Perhaps if we had not seen these personnel changes foisted upon us, or if you had arrived on time, but as it is," he spread his hands and concluded, "I certainly do not have the time, nor does anyone else."

"You expect me to start handling my responsibilities without any briefing?"

"Quite an impossibility, I most certainly agree." This time the air of satisfaction was unmistakable. Fernwhistle opened the first of two files on his desk and slid across a paper. "The first allotments of funds have already arrived, you see. We are all under tremendous pressure to release this money and begin the building process."

Jake glanced at the sheet, did a double take. There was a dollar sign, followed by a nine, and then a string of zeros. The sum hit him with an electric shock. It was one thing to hear Harry Grisholm talk about overseeing expenditures, the task kept at arm's length by time and distance. It was another thing entirely to be confronted with the actual *amount* and the responsibility of disbursing it. He gave a dry-lipped whistle.

"Just yesterday I had the deputy prime minister and the mayor of Istanbul both in here together," Fernwhistle told him, "demanding to know when I was going to release the apportionment. I simply must have immediate access to these funds."

"And you will," Jake replied steadily, "just as soon as I've had a chance to get my feet on the ground."

"Absolutely out of the question," Fernwhistle snapped. "This entire situation is preposterous. You were intended to answer not to me, nor to the consul general, but rather directly to this Mr. Grisholm, whoever he is. A man nobody knows, stationed five hundred miles away in Ankara, given direct responsibility for a staff member of this consulate." Fernwhistle snorted his derision. "A ridiculous arrangement. Now this Grisholm character is not even in the country. And his associate arrives here with no idea whatsoever of the pressures we are facing, then insists that the consulate set aside a thousand urgent issues just to bring him up to speed."

"Not the consulate," Jake replied, grimly holding on to his temper. "Just one person. If this is so all-fired important, somebody is bound to be able to spare me a little time."

"It would not be a *little* anything. This situation is vastly complicated. I have been here almost a year now, and I am just beginning to unravel the complexities." Again there was the faint glimmer of satisfaction. "I therefore insist that responsibility for these funds must pass from your hands to the consul general and from him to me."

"Insist anything you like," Jake replied evenly. "But until I hear something to the contrary from Harry Grisholm himself, things stand as they are."

"Out of the question! There is absolutely no way this absurd arrangement can be permitted to continue one moment longer. We simply must organize a proper chain of command." Fernwhistle opened the second folder and slid a typed document toward Jake. "Sign this, please."

Jake took in the embossed seal of the United States, read the heading, "Protocol of Authority," then looked up and asked, "What is this?"

"It simply confirms what I have been saying," Fernwhistle replied primly. "You are hereby granting me the authority to sign over whatever funds I deem are correct to the authorities in charge of the various projects."

Jake had to laugh. "You've sure got nerve, I'll grant you that."

Fernwhistle popped up like a marionette. "Now you look here, Burnes—"

"No." Jake heard the danger bells go off in his head. He rose to his feet, announced, "This meeting is over."

"The consul general will hear about this!"

"He sure will," Jake said, heading for the door.

"I assure you, Consul General Knowles will not look kindly upon your hindering this *crucial* work." Fernwhistle fairly danced out from behind his desk. He followed Jake toward the door with arms flapping, looking like an overgrown crane in a tailored gray suit. "If you stand in the way of this work, you'll be sent packing as fast as Gramble was."

Jake turned back and said as mildly as his ire would permit, "Seems to me, bub, the only one standing in the way of getting things done is you." He opened the door, said as an afterthought, "Now, why don't you just pack up all those papers and go find somebody who can start clarifying the situation."

He slammed the door behind him, took a fuming pair of steps, found himself almost colliding with the roly-poly figure of Ahmet, who announced, "Is already found."

Jake squinted down at the fat little man. "Say what?"

"The assistant to help with matters and understandings," Ahmet said with a beam. "Is waiting in your office."

"I'll just bet," Jake said, motioning with his chin for Ahmet to lead the way.

They went down one flight of stairs, passed along a broad corridor, and stopped at a doorway set within a narrow alcove. Ahmet opened the door with a flourish. "Is young Selim, at your service."

Jake entered a windowless chamber hardly larger than a broom closet. He nodded at the young man standing in the center of the chamber, then took in the dingy walls, the metal desk and matching filing cabinet, the pair of wooden chairs with peeling varnish, the utter lack of decoration. "They spared no expense, I see."

"Oh, is only outer office. Your office is through here." Ahmet bustled forward, opened the inner portal, motioned Jake through. "Please, please."

"The excitement can wait awhile," Jake decided, turning back to the young man. "Your name is Selim. Do I have that right?"

"Is Selim, yes, sir." He was as slender as Ahmet was rotund, with delicate olive features and expressive dark eyes. He stood confidently in an oversized suit jacket, mismatched trousers, and a white shirt without a tie.

Jake eased onto the corner of the desk and motioned Selim toward the nearest chair. "Take a seat, why don't you?"

"Is most kind." Selim slouched down, extended his legs, reached into his coat pocket, drew out a cigarette and lit it. "Can start with work tomorrow," he announced with the smoke.

Jake propped one arm across his chest, placed the

other up at his chin and tugged down the corners of his mouth. "Is that so?"

"Indeed, yes." Another puff, then, "Have made much sacrifice to present self at proper appointed time."

"I should be eternally grateful," Jake managed. "Maybe even offer you a couple of free days straight off so you can get yourself settled."

The dark head nodded thoughtfully. "With pay, of course."

Jake coughed discreetly. The shirkers he had known in the army had nothing on this guy. "So how much accounting do you know?"

The delicate brow furrowed. "Please?"

"You know, like how to balance books."

The hand and cigarette waved carelessly. "Books weigh different amounts, yes? Is need to balance?"

"You've got a point," Jake agreed thoughtfully. "Typing, shorthand?"

"Oh no," Selim replied, extending his arms proudly. "Hands very long."

"Perfect." Jake slid from his desk. "I'm sorry my wife wasn't here to meet you, Selim."

"Perhaps with time," the young man replied, rising languidly.

"You bet." Jake motioned toward the outer door. "Wait outside for a second, will you? I want to have a word with Ahmet here." When the door had closed behind the young man, Jake demanded, "Whose idea was this, anyway?"

"Fernwhistle, he say find you assistant," Ahmet declared proudly. "I find."

"Figures. You don't happen to know when the consul general is due back, do you?"

"Day after tomorrow," Ahmet replied promptly. "Selim is good boy, yes?"

"A great kid," Jake affirmed. "But he's not going to cut the mustard in this office."

The round forehead grew creases. "Please?"

"I want you to find me some alternatives," Jake said. "Put an ad in the paper, run a flyer, whatever you do around here. I want an assistant, male or female, who speaks fluent English, types, and has an accounting background. Shorthand is optional."

The creases deepened. "You no like Selim?"

Jake let a little of the edge he had been hiding come to the surface. "Did you get what I just said?"

"English, type, accounts," Ahmet replied, his traditional smile slipping a notch. "Will be most difficult, Meester Jake."

"Just put the word out, will you?" Jake said, turning for the door. "I'm going to see if I can find what they've done with my wife."

Chapter Four

They had been put up at the Pera Palace, a grand European-styled structure whose central lobby rose all the way to the six-story roof. Hand-wrought iron balustrades lined each of the inner halls, with carpets and matching drapes to muffle sound and add to the ancient feel. The creaking mahogany elevator was open and clanking and slow as molasses.

Jake scarcely had time to enter the room, hug Sally, and take in the lofty ceiling and overstuffed furniture and grand four-poster bed before there was a knock on the door. He opened it and took a step back at the sight of Jasmyn in an evening gown, her green eyes unreadable. Behind her, Pierre stood in formal dress whites, his features folded into an enormous scowl. Sally stepped up beside Jake. "What on earth?"

Pierre asked, "Can we interest you in attending a formal reception? It is being hosted here in the hotel by the Norwegian consulate."

"Swedish," Jasmyn corrected.

"Norway, Sweden, what difference could it make?"

"You've got to be kidding," Jake said, ushering them in.

"I wish that I was." Pierre stepped into the room,

said, "You are now looking at the new deputy military attaché to the French consulate."

"I thought you were supposed to be working with me."

"It appears the consul general had other ideas," Pierre replied.

"They had an argument," Jasmyn announced.

Sally asked, "You were there?"

Jasmyn shook her head. "I was waiting in Pierre's office."

"Which was on another floor," Pierre added, "at the opposite end of the building."

"Well, that beats my tale," Jake said. "I didn't have the guts to lose my temper."

Pierre eyed his friend. "You, too?"

Jake nodded. "You get the impression we're being railroaded?"

"All I can say for certain," Pierre said carefully, "is that the consular staff seem extremely concerned to keep me as busy doing nothing as they possibly can. Already I am assigned to attend conferences and receptions every day this week and the next."

Before Jake could respond, there was another knock at the door. Sally walked over, opened it, said, "Yes?"

A rich voice said, "I was wondering if a Colonel Burnes might be available."

"We need to be going," Pierre said.

"Stick around," Jake pleaded. "This may be my chance to make up for my poor showing back at the consulate."

An older gentleman entered the room. His appearance was grandfatherly, his gaze keen. "Colonel Burnes? I'm Tom Knowles."

Jake stiffened. "The consul general?"

"That's right." He motioned behind him and was joined by a tall corpulent man in a rumpled suit. "This is Barry Edders, my political analyst."

"I thought you weren't back until the day after tomorrow."

"We're not," Edders agreed cheerfully. "He's not here, and we haven't met."

"I needed to get to you before attention turned your way and the avenues were closed off." He turned his steel-gray eyes toward Pierre. "You must be Major Servais."

"At your service, m'sieur." He motioned to Jasmyn. "My wife."

"And this is Sally Burnes," Jake added.

"Pleased to meet you." The consul general gave a swift but cordial nod before returning his attention to Jake. "It's good I caught you both together. This may be our only chance to speak freely, at least for a while." He glanced at his watch. "I'm afraid we don't have much time."

"We don't have any time at all," Edders agreed, his cheerfulness untouched by the consul general's serious tone. "Which doesn't matter, of course, since we're not really here."

"Won't you gentlemen sit down?" Sally offered.

"Thank you. As Barry has just said, this meeting is not taking place. It is imperative that we seem to be at odds with you both, but I really must speak with you openly. So I have decided to risk using the Swedish consular reception downstairs as a smoke screen and come here. This may be our only chance."

Jake motioned for everyone to find chairs, seated himself beside Sally on the sofa, and demanded, "Because we're not going to be around that long?"

"That may well be the case," Knowles admitted. "Hard to say at this point, however. For the time being, you are here, and faced with a situation that is growing more difficult with every passing day. You are aware that the funds have begun to arrive from Washington?"

"I saw the transcript upstairs in Mr. Fernwhistle's office."

"That was actually the third transfer. Ah, I see he failed to tell you that. No wonder. Yes, the first two arrived after the former consul general departed and prior to my own arrival. Acting on authority passed down by a very harried DCM in Ankara, Fernwhistle took it upon himself to dispense the initial funds."

"DCM stands for Deputy Chief of Mission in diplomatese," Barry explained easily, slouched far down in his chair. He seemed content to sit and chat all night. Whatever tension the others might be feeling did not faze him in the least. "He's number two at the embassy in Ankara. Whenever the ambassador is away, the DCM rules the roost."

"Precisely," Knowles agreed. "But with this initial disbursement, Fernwhistle found himself possessing power and influence on a breathtaking scale, something rarely experienced by a diplomat at his level."

Pierre demanded, "What about bribes, kickbacks?"

"Not Fernwhistle," the consul general replied definitely. "I've worked with him before, and I know him to be an honest diplomat, quite diligent in his own somewhat limited way."

"Not enough imagination," Barry agreed easily. "He's so clean he squeaks. Now if it were me in that situation—"

"Which it is not and never will be," Knowles responded, his eyes never leaving Jake. "But there is more to this than just some second-tier Foreign Service official out for his own taste of glory."

"I sort of figured that," Jake said quietly.

"Of course you did. There are actually two battles going on. Fernwhistle is the tip of one iceberg, which is the struggle over who is going to control this outlay of funds. State Department wants it, as does the Pentagon, not to mention the fact that numerous White House officials are weighing in personally. You are simply facing the field skirmish in a vicious turf war back in Washington." He glanced at Pierre, added, "I fear you shall face much the same difficulty from your own officials, Major."

"I already have," Pierre replied.

"Sorry to hear that." He turned back to Jake. "For the moment, because of the Soviet Union's interest in Turkey, the military has been assigned equal status, which of course is why you are here. And which brings up the second battle." Knowles leaned back, lines of weariness suddenly appearing about his mouth and eyes. "Why don't you take over, Barry."

"Right." The political officer made a futile attempt at straightening the lapels of his jacket and began, "You're aware of the struggle to get the United Nations up and running?"

"As much as the next guy, I guess."

"In that crisis you can see a concentration of everything we're facing here. On the one hand, we're trying to deal with the Russians as allies and let them have a hand in the UN and everything else that has resulted from our victory. On the other, we're being forced to accept that Stalin's Russia is just about the biggest threat our nation has ever faced. And Russia's been trying to get its hands on Turkey for centuries." Despite the bleakness of his news, the buoyant attitude never slipped a notch. "I guarantee you, Colonel, you'll never come across a more confounded mess in all your born days."

"Call me Jake."

"Right. There's no clear-cut agreement on this problem, not by the boyos sitting in their comfy offices back in Washington. Of course, everybody who's been up close to the front lines agrees that the Soviets are a menace and that they're on the march. But actual evidence is hard to come by. On the surface, these Russkies are all bonhomie and back-slapping."

"I've just experienced a little of that firsthand," Jake said and described their meeting with Dimitri Kolonov.

"Yeah, that Dimitri is a piece of work. I've already gotten the word on him from a buddy back in Sofia. You'll find a lot of them like that, so slick you can't keep a grip on them with pliers and a noose. But mark my words, they're up to no good."

"You think," Knowles corrected.

"I know," Barry insisted comfortably. "I just haven't managed to get my hands on the evidence to convince the rubber-stampers back in Washington."

"Those are our superiors you are referring to," Knowles chided, but there was no condemnation to his tone.

"Yeah, well, this meeting didn't ever take place, so I guess it really doesn't matter what I don't say."

"Then what you need from me," Jake said, "is help finding something to pin the Russians down with."

"I heard about your escapade up in Berlin," Barry acknowledged. "Sounded like quite a time was had by all. I told Tom here about it, and he decided to risk this meeting."

"Officially we will have to be on opposite sides of the fence," Knowles reiterated gravely. "At least unless or until State and Defense can iron out their differences."

"Or until I'm replaced," Jake interjected.

"Let us hope that does not happen, Colonel. I feel certain we would work well together." Knowles rose to his feet. "Unofficially, if there is anything you need, anything at all, I want you to discuss it with Barry. He will bring it up with me."

"We're not allowed to talk with you," Barry explained. "But everybody's sort of given me up as a lost cause. So long as you keep your visits down to a few minutes at a time and not too frequent, I can run interference for you."

"Thanks, I guess."

Knowles extended his hand. "Make no mistake, Colonel. Your work is absolutely vital to America's future interests in this part of the world. But sorting out the conflicts between politicians who still see the Russians as friends and those who see them as our single greatest enemy will take some time and a good deal more hard evidence. Remember, any number of senior officials back in Washington have built their careers upon the fact that Russia has been an important ally throughout the war. We must be patient and work together to convince them that times have changed, and changed drastically."

Knowles's grip was as steady and strong as his gaze. "Mark my words. The confrontation in Berlin was not some isolated incident, but the herald of things to come."

Chapter Five

The next day, Jake entered the consulate grounds to find a courtyard flooded with people. Ahmet greeted him at the door and announced with his great, beaming smile, "Is people wishing to apply for position of assistant, Meester Jake."

Jake turned and looked back over the assembled throng. "All of them?"

"Ahmet do just what you say, Meester Jake, look high and low for good assistant."

He looked doubtfully at the little man. "All of them have been vetted? They are all qualified?"

"Oh, most certainly yes, Meester Jake." He took in the courtyard with a proud sweep of his arm. "These the best you find." He dropped his arm, stepped closer, said more quietly, "Unless, of course, you are accepting Selim as assistant."

"Out of the question," Jake said, turning for the door. "I'll see them in my office. Have them come up one at a time."

The line of applicants seemed endless. All had dark complexions and finely sculpted features, male and female alike. All spoke English in varying shades and disguises. Some used a grammar so convoluted Jake was positive they had learned it from an outdated book, without aid of a teacher. These applicants he treated with great respect, for there are few endeavors more difficult, or more indicative of determination and intelligence, than learning a new language alone. Yet none of them had any experience with accounting, and few could even type.

Some applicants had an accent so heavy they might as well have been speaking another tongue. Jake smiled his way through these interviews, asking a few polite questions, explaining carefully that he was under pressure to get up and running and so needed someone with an absolute and total grasp of English. He was not sure they understood him any better than he did them.

Throughout the entire day, Ahmet remained in Jake's outer office. The obsequious man smoked so many of his foul cigarettes that every time Jake opened his door he was struck by a billowing cloud.

Halfway through the afternoon, the phone in Jake's office rang for the first time, startling him almost out of his seat. Tentatively he lifted the antiquated receiver, heard a series of pops and hisses and static squeals, said repeated hellos with increasing volume.

Suddenly through the static came a familiar voice. "Jake, is that you?"

"Harry?" He made frantic hand motions for Ahmet to usher out the next incoming applicant and to close the door. "Where are you?"

"London. Good grief, this line is awful. Can you hear me?"

"Barely."

"Well, it will have to do. I've been trying to get through since yesterday. And that, mind you, with every ounce of political pressure I could bring to bear."

Jake raised his voice, shouted, "When do you arrive?"

"That's the problem. I still don't know. I would swear that there are unseen forces at work here."

Jake looked over at his now-closed door, said, "I can imagine."

"Eh, what was that? You'll have to speak up, man."

"There have been developments here too," Jake said.

"No doubt. Kolonov has introduced himself?"

"In a manner of speaking."

"You got my message then. Good. I assume I do not need to discuss with you the matter of security."

"Or trust."

"Exactly. You may assume that every wall has ears, and there are a dozen listeners to every spoken word."

Including the present conversation, Jake understood. "I sure could use a friend close at hand."

"I shall arrive at the soonest possible opportunity, I assure you. In the meantime, there is always the chance of our turning this situation to our advantage and learning what we can."

"I'm afraid I'm in over my head," Jake confessed, this time not caring who heard.

"Nonsense." Harry Grisholm's confidence managed to pass over the crackling line. "There is no one else I would rather have watching out for our interests, Jake."

"Shows how misguided even the experts can be," Jake said, but found himself smiling in spite of himself.

"Look for allies in unexpected places, that's my advice. You always were one for landing on your feet. I count on you to do nothing less there in Istanbul."

"A few allies," Jake said, "would be a welcome addition."

"Go beyond the normal routine, then. Examine avenues which are overlooked by the ones wearing blinders."

"Hard to find those avenues," Jake replied, "when I can't even read the street signs."

"A joke. Good. I like that." The exuberance refused to be contained by the static-filled line. "Now as to the funds."

"The third allocation arrived yesterday," Jake said, glancing over to the closed folder. So many zeros. "It boggles the mind, Harry."

"Our job is to make sure it is money well spent. If you are not satisfied about anything, then wait. Delay payment. Demand better details. Ask questions. Inspect in person. We must be sure that these initial actions follow correct procedures."

"Easier said than done."

"You are experiencing pressure?"

"From all sides."

"And I am not there to protect your back." A somber briskness pressed on. "Well, it simply cannot be helped. You must be strong, my friend. And stubborn." The line faded away entirely, then came back with a shouted, "Jake? Are you there?"

"Still here," he yelled.

"I am losing you. Take care, my friend. I shall join you as soon as I can. And remember—" But the line chose that moment to go dead.

Slowly Jake replaced the receiver, feeling more isolated and distant from protected waters than at any time since the war.

• • •

By six o'clock his head felt as if it were full of used chewing gum, and he was no closer to finding an assistant. Wearily he smiled and shook another hand and ushered another applicant out. He leaned on the doorpost and said, "I'm positive I asked for someone with accounting experience."

"Was no good, Meester Jake?"

Jake looked down at Ahmet's beaming face and the oily strands of hair plastered down tight over the gleaming skull. "Mr. Burnes, Jake, Colonel, Colonel Burnes. All of them are fine. This Meester Jake business has got to go."

Ahmet nodded, all smiles. "Was not the ideal candidate?"

"Ideal is somewhere on the other side of the moon. I'm not searching for ideal. I just want someone who can add, subtract, and tell me the result in an English I can understand." Jake examined Ahmet and said for the dozenth time that day, "I thought you said you had vetted these candidates."

"Oh yes, most careful vetting," Ahmet agreed. "This last lady, she was very pretty, no?"

"Grand. Just grand. Only I don't see how a background as a music teacher and two courses in French prepare her to be my assistant."

Ahmet made grave eyes. "She was not mathematics teacher? She did not live in England?"

Jake had to laugh. "When I showed her the rows of numbers, she looked like they were going to reach out and bite her. And I'm still not sure how it was we communicated at all, since I don't speak any Turkish, and I am pretty sure she's never been anywhere within shouting distance of an English dictionary, much less England."

"Oh, oh, oh." Ahmet gave his head a mournful shake. "Is so hard to find worthy employees in such times." He paused for a moment of sober reflection, then brightened. "Perhaps you should speak yet again with young Selim?"

"I believe I'm finally beginning to get the picture," Jake replied. "The mist is finally clearing before my eyes. Selim wouldn't happen to be a relative of yours, would he?"

"Oh no, Meester Jake. Not mine. Sister's husband's nephew." The patented beam returned. "Is very nice boy."

"Your very nice boy can't add, thinks subtraction is something to do with his fingers and toes, and wrestles with English almost as well as I do with alligators." Jake pushed himself erect. "Bring on the next candidate."

Ahmet opened pudgy palms toward the ceiling. "Is no more."

"That's all?" Jake had to smile at the man's audacity. "You've scoured the streets and filled my day with twenty-three people who don't know accounting from acrobatics, and you say that's the best you can do?"

"Is terrible, no?" The beam widened. "Perhaps you see Selim tomorrow after all."

"Highly unlikely." Jake found himself not minding in the least when a glint of exasperation showed on the little man's face. He reached for his coat, shut and locked his door, turned back to see Ahmet struggling to recapture his grin. "We'll start again tomorrow."

"But Meester Jake—"

"Accountants," Jake said, stopping him with a hand

that pushed at the air between them so hard the little man squeaked back a step. "Accountants with English. Remember that. And don't waste any more of my time."

His anger and his fatigue powered him down the stairs and through the lobby so swiftly that he was already beside the Marine's desk before the oddity struck home. He turned for another glance, saw that there was indeed a thin, bearded man hunched in the corner of the corridor's only bench. It was very strange, for security measures forbade anyone inside the front door without an escort.

Jake leaned over the Marine's barrier and faced the young man who had brought them in from the train station the day before. For the life of him, his fatigue-addled brain could not come up with the soldier's name. "Who's he waiting to see, Corporal?"

"Why, you, sir."

Jake glanced from the tired, disheveled-looking man on the bench to the Marine and back again. "Say that again?"

"He was the first applicant to be passed through this morning." The young man was typical of the consular guard staff, spit-shined and erect and so fresh he made Jake feel ancient. "Mrs. Ecevit vetted him personally."

Jake searched his memory, came up with another vague recollection from the day before. "Let's see, she's aide to the political officer, do I have that right?"

"That's the one." The Marine hesitated, then said, "Sir, is it true what they say, that you were in the push through Italy and all?"

"That was a long time ago, soldier. Another lifetime."

But the Marine wasn't finished. "And that story about you rescuing the French resistance officer and carrying him through the desert? And what about you getting behind the Russkie lines and sneaking out those scientists and helping to start up the Berlin airlift?"

Jake gaped at the young man. "Where on earth did you hear all that guff?"

"From the Frenchie, sir, I mean Major Servais. He talked about you the whole way to the hotel yesterday. Your wife too. The major stopped by here this morning, but when he saw the line of people waiting to see you, he hung around a little, talking with us here at the station, then took off."

The young man could no longer suppress his grin. "The stories are all true, aren't they, sir? Boy, wait until the other guys hear about this. The major said you won the Silver Star and the Croix de Guerre, had that one pinned on by DeGaulle himself, I guess that's true too, sir?"

Jake started to brush off the admiration, then found himself staring into those clear gray eyes and wondering if perhaps he had found himself an unexpected ally. "Do you know this Mrs. Ecevit personally?"

"Oh yes, sir." The Marine bounced to full attention at the chance to offer more than polite chitchat. "I've been here almost a year now. I guess I know everybody, at least enough to say hello."

"What can you tell me about her?"

"She's a real firecracker, sir." The grin was hard to keep trapped, even at attention. "Sharp as a tack, too. I've seen her lay into that Ahmet fellow right back there in the corridor, peel skin from bone better than my drill sergeant back on Parris Island."

"She did?" The woman's stock just shot up. "You know why?"

"No, but I can guess. She doesn't have time for pencil pushers and official sneaks, sir."

"She doesn't."

"Not a second." A glance around the empty hall, then, "A guy who keeps his eyes open can see a lot from here, sir. That Ahmet's always scampering around, sticking his nose where it doesn't belong, sucking up to the guys with perks and power."

"I've noticed."

"Sure, I mean, yessir. Anyway, I imagine he tried it once too often with the lady, and she proceeded to blister his hide." A flicker of movement out of the corner, and the Marine snapped to rigid alert, finished with a crisp, "Sir."

A deeper voice said, "Can I help you with anything, Colonel?"

Jake turned to face the guard sergeant, a stern-faced leatherneck with four rows of campaign ribbons. Jake nodded a greeting. "Just getting to know one of your men a little. Hope that's all right."

"Long as he sticks to his duty, I suppose it's okay, sir."

"Thank you," Jake said, playing at ease. "What's your name, Sergeant?"

"Adams, sir." A half-made salute, just enough in the gesture and the eyes to let Jake know he was not going to curry favor with anyone. He was far beyond either the need or the desire.

Jake decided it was worth meeting the man head on. He glanced down at the ribbons, found two he recognized. "You were at Anzio?"

"That's right." The gaze sharpened. "What about you?"

Jake shook his head. "Came ashore at Syracuse. Met some of your group outside Naples. Tough assignment."

"Yeah, ain't they all?" The rigid reserve relaxed a notch. "There's been a French officer around here this morning, you catch his name, Bailey?"

"Major Servais, sir." The young Marine officer bit off the words.

"That's the one. He had some pretty interesting tales to tell, Colonel. Any of 'em true?"

"Old war stories grow like fish caught yesterday," Jake replied. "They get bigger with each telling."

The measuring gaze granted him a hint of approval. "Now, ain't that the truth."

Jake decided it was time to plant a seed. He leaned over the guardpost barrier, said quietly, "You soldiers know what it means to be a duck out of water?"

Within the sergeant's steely gaze appeared a glinting blade of humor. "We're here, ain't we?"

"I've been pulled from garrison duty at Badenburg, given a grand total of three weeks' training," Jake said, stretching the truth a mite, "then thrown out here and told to do the impossible."

The sergeant glanced at the Marine. "Sounds just like the corps, don't it, Bailey?"

"Sure does, Sarge."

"What's your first name, Corporal?" Jake demanded.

"Samuel. Samuel Bailey, sir."

Jake nodded, as though taking the news in deep, giving it value. Then back to the sergeant. "I need use of your eyes and your ears, Sergeant. Yours and your men's."

Back to the measuring gaze. "This a formal requisition, Colonel?"

"If it is," Jake replied, "then no matter how tight I try to keep it, sooner or later it's going to become common knowledge. Two days here, and I'm already aware of that."

A single chop of a nod in agreement. "The political officer appears to be a guy who doesn't leave a paper trail."

"You want me to let somebody else know we've talked," Jake said, understanding him, and taking great comfort from the fact that he had suggested Barry Edders. "I don't have any trouble with that at all. Tomorrow I'll lay it out." He let a little of his fatigue and his desperation show through. "I've got to find some people I can trust, Sergeant. And fast. I'm not asking for anything in particular. Just to keep watch and let me know what's on the up and up."

"Help you find the bear traps and the land mines," the sergeant offered.

"That's it exactly."

The sergeant glanced at the soldier standing duty. "I don't see as how I've got a problem with that. What about you, Bailey?"

"It'd be an honor, sir. I'm sure I can speak for all the guys. A genuine honor."

Jake dropped his eyes in an attempt to mask the relief he felt. But he looked to find the sergeant's steady gaze looking deep and had to say, "You don't know what that means, finding somebody I can rely on. My back is truly to the wall."

The leatherneck broke the hardness of his face

enough to offer a quick thin-lipped smile. "Any chance of some action, Colonel? This guard duty starts to weigh heavy after a while."

"I would say there is a good chance of that," Jake replied, and then was struck with an idea. "How'd you like me to see if the consul general would assign one of you fellows to travel up country with me? Could be dangerous, though."

That brought a reaction so strong Jake felt he was watching the sun appear from behind heavy cloud cover. "You just said the magic words, Colonel. Travel and danger."

"I'll speak with somebody first thing tomorrow morning," Jake promised. He nodded at their crisp salutes, the sergeant's now as snappy as the corporal's. Then he turned back to the corridor. "And thanks."

He walked over to where the bearded man sat slouched upon the bench. The eyes did not rise at Jake's approach. Jake slowed, took the time to inspect the man more closely. His black suit, shiny with age, hung limply upon his bony frame. The scraggly beard was laced with gray threads. A battered and dusty fedora rested in the man's lap.

Jake sat down on the bench, watched as the man emerged slowly from his stooped reverie and lifted hollowed cheeks and dark eyes to stare back. Then for a moment Jake found himself unable to speak. The sight of that ever-hungry gaze drew him back to another time, when he had stood outside a barbed-wire compound and watched the haggard faces of war stare back. He swallowed, managed, "They told me all the applicants had been seen."

The man continued to watch him for a moment, then replied in softly accented English, "It is the way

of people such as your Mr. Ahmet. They will grant me
entry, then leave me seated here for as long as I am
willing to remain and endure the silent humiliation.
Then, you see, they are able to claim that they have
never practiced discrimination. It is a most Turkish of
solutions."

Jake nodded slowly, "You are Jewish?"

"I am." The steady gaze faltered, and one pale hand
lifted to cover his eyes. "Forgive me. I should not have
spoken as I did. But I have been waiting here . . ."

"Since early this morning. I just heard from the
guard. I am sorry. That is unforgivable."

"It is expected." The hand dropped tiredly. "But I
decided to try, nonetheless, even though it was known
that all consulates are closed shops, with local employment controlled by one such as Ahmet."

"He's obviously let one slip through his grasp. Mrs.
Ecevit."

"Indeed. A friend of my mother, the only reason I
learned of your need for an assistant. She was hired by
the political officer while Mr. Ahmet was out sick. She
is a breach of his little empire which will not be permitted to last. Something will happen, some unforgivable accident or theft or loss or passage of information
to the enemy. And it will be traced back to Mrs. Ecevit.
There will be no question, none whatsoever, who is re-
sponsible."

"Not," Jake replied grimly, "if I have anything to do
about it."

The bearded man gave a tired, tolerant smile. "You
have entered a country with almost forty percent un-
employment. The power to give someone a job is
greater than that of having money. Your Mr. Ahmet
will not be pried loose easily, Mr. . . ."

He offered his hand. "Burnes. Jake Burnes."

"Daniel Levy."

The man's grip was cool and firm. Jake felt a sudden urging, said, "Levi. The tribe of priests. The ones granted no province of their own, but rather cities within all the other tribes' lands."

The veil of fatigue lifted from the man's gaze. "You have studied the Torah?"

"The Bible," Jake replied.

"Ah. You are Christian."

"Yes."

"I do not use the word as a description of your heritage."

"No," Jake agreed. "Nor I."

There was a slow nod, one which took hold of the man's entire upper body, back and forth in measured pace. "You are far from home, Mr. Burnes."

"Very far," Jake agreed. "Where did you learn your English?"

"Here and there," the man said, his offhand manner suggesting he was still caught by Jake's earlier admission.

"Do you speak other languages?"

A continuation of the same slow nod. "Turkish, of course. And Greek. My nanny spoke no other language. And my family spoke mostly French within the home. That and Ladino."

"Come again?"

A hesitant smile parted the strands of his beard. "Perhaps that is a story that should wait for another time."

"What work experience have you had?"

A hesitation, a strange sense of regret, then, "Until the last year of the war I was employed by a large local company as their accountant."

"You don't say." Jake felt the thrill of discovery. "And since then?"

The regret solidified into gaunt lines. "How long have you been in this country, Mr. Burnes?"

"A grand total," Jake replied, "of two days."

"I regret that to answer your question I must reveal one of my country's more shameful mistakes."

"A camp," Jake breathed. "They put you in a concentration camp."

Dark eyes inspected him closely. "You have seen the death camps?"

"Some of the survivors," Jake replied. "As close as I ever want to come."

"This was nothing so horrendous," Daniel Levy stated. "But bad enough, nonetheless. Turkey held grimly to its noncombatant status, as did Switzerland. But we are far larger than Switzerland, with eight times the population and even more land mass. Germany continued to push the Turkish government into declaring itself a Nazi ally. Two of the most strongly worded directives were to supply Germany with troops and to round up the Jewish population. Turkey made the first small step to obey just eleven months before the war finally ended, when Germany threatened to lose its patience and invade."

The consulate's cool marble entrance hall was no place for this pale gentleman and his quietly suffering voice and his story. Jake said, "You don't have to tell me this."

"The government issued a proclamation," Daniel Levy continued in his soft voice, speaking to the opposite wall. "Male Jews over the age of eighteen were rounded up and taken to camps. The soldiers who came for us were most polite and regretful. I remember that one sergeant even saluted me as I stepped into the truck. I also remember how the lieutenant driving our truck told us to take a good look, because if the Germans came any closer to our borders we would not see our homes again."

Jake took in the words, the pallid features, the waxy long-fingered hands, the unkempt beard, the lost gaze. "And still you call this your country."

"Some are now leaving, those with relatives elsewhere, especially in America. Others are speaking of new beginnings in Israel. But my family has lived in Istanbul for almost five hundred years. We have lived in our home for seven generations. I, my father, his father before him, and his before that, all were married in the same synagogue." Dark eyes turned with resigned sorrow to Jake. "Tell me, Mr. Burnes, if we were to leave, who would remain to keep our heritage alive?"

"I understand," Jake said. He planted his hands on his knees, asked, "Can you type?"

"Some." The man's gaze was questioning. "Why?"

Jake had heard enough. The emotion drawn from Daniel Levy's responses was too raw for him to do more than stand, offer his hand, and ask, "Can you start tomorrow?"

Chapter Six

Y ou don't waste time, do you?"
Jake slid into the seat opposite Barry Edders'
cluttered desk. "I'm a little short of extra minutes."

"Yeah I suppose that's so." Even first thing in the
morning, the political officer's cheery manner was sol-
idly in place. "So you want me to talk with the CG, let
him know you'd like to enlist our marines to your little
effort."

"Just borrow them from time to time, is all."

"Well, I don't have any problem with that. Don't
guess the CG will, either." He shuffled through a hap-
hazard pile of papers, came up with a relatively clean
sheet, scribbled on one edge. "Anything else?"

"Yes, as a matter of fact." Jake had spent much of
the previous night planning this discussion. Keeping
their talks to a minimum meant getting as much from
each one as possible.

"Figured there would be." Barry sighed contentedly as he propped his shoes upon the desk's corner.
He sipped his coffee, waved the mug in Jake's general
direction. "Sure I can't offer you some?"

"I'm fine, thanks. I need—"

"You'll learn soon enough never to pass up a

chance for a decent cup," Barry said, sliding down a bit further in the chair, getting himself truly comfortable. "The local stuff tastes like wet sand."

"I've had Arabic coffee before." Jake cocked his head to one side. "Do you ever let anything bother you?"

"Used to." Another sip, taking it slow, breathing in the steam, sighing at the flavor. Savoring the moment. "You see any action, Jake?"

"You mean, in the war? Some."

"Me, too. Philippines, Okinawa, Tinian. Political science professor one day, captain of infantry the next." He took another contented sip, glancing back over his shoulder at the sunlight that streamed in through his floor-to-ceiling windows, said mildly, "There couldn't have been, oh, more than a couple dozen times when I scraped through by the skin of my teeth."

"I know the feeling," Jake said quietly. "All too well."

"Way I see it," Barry went on, turning back to the room, "every day's a gift. My job is to enjoy it as much as I can. I love my work, love being overseas, love serving my country. I just can't let any of the memories or any of the current pressures get between me and appreciating the gift of life." Another thoughtful sip. "Or between me and my God."

"Faith has helped me a lot," Jake said carefully. "But I'll never get to where you are. Not in a thousand years."

"Yeah, I thought maybe you and your wife were believers." He snatched up another sheet of paper, scribbled busily, then passed it over, all without shifting either shoes or cup. "Address of the church where a lot of the expatriate community worships. Good place. You'd be most welcome."

"Thanks," Jake said, and suddenly found it necessary to duck his head and hide how much the simple gesture meant to him just then.

"We're cut from two different stalks, you and I," Barry went on. "My way of dealing with the world suits who I am. Same with you."

"It doesn't mean," Jake said, lifting his gaze, "that I couldn't learn from you. A lot."

Barry eyed him thoughtfully over the rim of his mug, then said, "I hope the situation changes, Jake, and gives us the chance to become friends."

"Maybe we already are," Jake replied.

"Yeah, maybe you're right at that." The brisk cheerfulness returned. "So what else can I do for you this morning?"

"I need all the accounts and correspondence dealing with the first two outlays of funds."

"That ought to stick a feather up old Fernwhistle's nose." Barry grinned as he scribbled a note. "Consider it done. Anything else?"

"A car and driver. Available day and night, short notice, maybe no notice at all. Somebody competent, safe, and able to keep his trap shut."

"Competent and safe are words that don't exist on Turkish roads. Confidential isn't a problem, though. These guys are so grateful for a job they wouldn't dream of yapping." Another scribble. "Car will be placed at your disposal day and night, driver available days only unless you give prior notice. See Sergeant Adams for how the roster works. What else?"

"Keep Ahmet off my back."

Barry grinned. "Heard about your little escapade

with the hiring process. Pretty neat the way you did the end run on him."

"Why do you put up with him?"

"I don't, personally. As to the others," Barry shrugged. "You got to remember, most of the Americans here have had years experience back in Washington learning how not to make waves. Most of them are so grateful for the chance to serve overseas they'd eat a yard of wet laundry to keep the job."

"That guy is a menace."

"Yeah, well, I could push my weight around, but if I do, I'd tip our hand. So I'm going to have to let you handle this one on your own."

"Thanks a million."

"Hey, what are pals for, right?" An easy grin across the desk, then, "Anything else?"

"Just one point. I'd like to meet with your assistant."

"You want to spend time with Mrs. Ecevit?" For once, Barry registered genuine surprise. "Why?"

"You're not supposed to be asking me that," Jake said. "You were the one who hired her."

"Oh, don't get me wrong. She's fantastic. But she's also fairly high up the hard-to-handle scale. My two staffers call her Mrs. Prickly Pear. Personally, I love her mind, but not her attitude." He waited, granting Jake a chance to opt out. When he did not, Barry continued to press the point home. "Even I prefer to keep her at arm's length and receive everything she has to say in writing."

But Jake had already made up his mind. "I'll take my chances, if it's all right with you."

"Be my guest. She's off doing some work for me just now, but she should be back after lunch." A grand smile creased his features as he turned away. "Just don't say I didn't warn you."

"Are you sure this is it?"

Sally glanced from the note in her hand to the brass plaque set upon the tall entrance gate. "Rosewood Bungalow. See for yourself."

Jasmyn peered doubtfully at the great stone edifice rising beyond the formal gardens. "This is a bunga-low?"

"Somebody's idea of a joke, more likely." Sally started forward. "If it is, she's in for a nasty surprise. My well of good humor is just about all run dry."

The previous day had been spent inspecting the apartments assigned the two couples. Jasmyn had al-most wept at the sight of hers; when it came to Sally's turn, she could not help but laugh.

Pierre and Jasmyn had been assigned a two-room apartment in a rundown central-city tenement. The French consulate had dumped so much furniture and fittings inside that there was scarcely room for one per-son to walk about, much less for two people to start a life together. The apartment was on the second floor above a busy street; with the continual din below, they had to shout to hear each other. The single small bal-cony overlooked a central courtyard of cracked cement and weeds and a dirt-filled fountain. There was no sunlight or sky at all, the view totally blocked by clotheslines strung from higher balconies. Along with the bedlam of crying babies and screaming children and screeching mothers came the continual sound of dripping water. The air stank of starch and cheap detergent.

Sally's apartment was equally ridiculous, but on the opposite end of the scale. The pre-war building occupied an entire city block. She had opened the door to discover a residence spanning the entire floor. The paltry bits of furniture supplied by the consulate had only amplified the cavernous depths. Their exploration had taken on the air of a trek, calling out to each other to find their way back together, their footsteps echoing loudly from wooden floors and distant ceilings. There were six bathrooms and nine fireplaces. Nine. The kitchen was larger than Jasmyn's entire apartment.

Without further ado, they had commandeered two baffled drivers and cars from the French consulate and spent the remainder of the day shifting every stick of furniture from Jasmyn's apartment to Sally's. That evening they had pumped each other up, ready to do battle with both men for the right to live together. To their astonishment, neither had offered any argument whatsoever. Jake had seemed relieved. Pierre had said little, but had given the impression that they would probably not be around long enough to need to worry over accommodations. His entire second day had been spent in further explosive encounters.

Then the note had arrived with Sally's breakfast tray.

Sally was growing restless to move out of the hotel and into something more settled. She had no complaints about the hotel itself, other than the feeling that eyes followed her everywhere and privacy had become a relative term. Even room service was losing its appeal. Sally had slipped open the note, read the brief invitation to morning coffee, then gone to fetch Jasmyn.

Together they walked up the long winding drive, past ancient rosebushes trained to climb over a variety of surfaces. Rose-covered fountains sprayed musical water. Heavy stone walls were almost lost beneath their burden of blooming vines. Ancient trees and even older Roman columns were surrounded by trellises, upon which roses had been trained to grow and bloom in profusion.

"Oh, how simply marvelous. You must be Mrs. Burnes."

Sally stopped, searched, could not locate the source of the voice. "That's right."

"And right spot on time." A elderly face lifted above a rose-clad embankment and beamed at them. She wore a wide-brimmed straw hat and a smile as brilliant as the morning sun. "No mean feat, in these uncertain realms."

"Mrs. Hollamby?"

"Call me Phyllis, won't you, my dear? It's so much smaller a mouthful." She rose to her feet with the help of a sturdy cane, stripped off her gardening gloves, tottered over. "And you must be Mrs. Servais."

"Call me Jasmyn, please."

"Such a lovely name, it would be a pleasure." Bright eyes peered from a friendly face. "And the name matches the lady, I must say. Two enchanting guests for coffee, how splendid." She brushed at the dirt staining her simple cotton shift. "Just look at this, would you? Such a mess. I do so apologize, but it is so very difficult to keep track of time when I am out in my garden. You must think me terribly rude."

"I've always felt that was one of the nice things about gardening," Sally replied. "Having a perfect excuse to get good and messy."

"What a charming thought." She peered at Sally a moment longer, then nodded as though having reached a decision. "I have ordered coffee to be served in the garden. It's so pleasant this time of day."

The table was sheltered by a rose-covered trellis and layered in starched linen. It supported a silver coffee service and settings for three. Jasmyn exclaimed, "This is beautiful."

"Thank you, my dear. Yes, mornings are positively delightful out here. By midafternoon, however, I fear the atmosphere can be a bit overpowering. Roses seem to give out more scent with heat, or perhaps it is that so many summer days here are windless." She settled herself like an aging dowager and said to Sally, "Perhaps you would be kind enough to pour."

"I'd be happy to." As she steadied the heavy pot, she said, "Mrs. Fothering told us it was important that we try to meet with you."

"Yes, she has been kind enough to inform me of your little encounter." Sky-blue eyes twinkled merrily. "And of your meeting with our little friends the governess and her Swiss companion."

Sally tried to match the woman's light tone, though it cost her. "She said we were in grave danger."

Phyllis gave a gay peal of laughter, and the years positively melted away. "I would not pay overmuch attention to such blatherings, if I were you, my dear."

Sally felt a rush of relief so strong it left her weak. "But they were so, well, convincing."

"Deadly serious," Jasmyn added.

"Well, they would be, wouldn't they? I mean, that is why our Mrs. Fothering did not inform them of her own purpose on the journey, which was to see if they were worthy of joining our little band. Nor have they been told what role I myself play." She took a delicate sip, went on, "You see, my dear, there are those among us who feel they can give greater merit to their deeds by filling their little worlds with unnecessary drama."

Sally sank back in her seat and glanced at an equally restored Jasmyn. "Then Jake and Pierre aren't in danger after all."

"Why, of course they are, my dear." Phyllis Hollamby smiled brightly. "They are gathering intelligence in Turkey. There could scarcely be a more perilous occupation in all the world."

"But you said—"

Mrs. Hollamby reached over and patted Sally's hand. "I simply said that these women and their melodrama were out of place. Such ladies like to fill their lives with commotion. That is their choice. But to instill unnecessary ferment in the heart of a newcomer is, well, excuse me for saying it, but it really is simply balderdash." She looked from one to the other and aligned her features before saying sternly, "Now, you really cannot allow yourselves to take this so seriously. All the world is full of peril. Both your husbands have lived to wear their well-earned decorations because they are experts at the art of survival. If you wish to assist them with this next challenge, you must begin by being alert and calm and steady."

"That's what we had decided as well," Sally told her.

"Well of course you have. From all reports, you're

both cut from proper staunch cloth." She looked from one young woman to the other. "I must tell you, what we have heard of your own war records has impressed our group enormously."

Jasmyn glanced in Sally's direction, then asked, "You know about us?"

"Oh my, yes. Otherwise we would have watched and waited before making contact. We must be extremely careful, you see. As to how, well, let us simply say for the moment that our network has extended at a most remarkable rate. People are relocated, and they take both the work and their desire to participate with them. New connections are made, new little circles started."

"That's what you call yourselves? Circles?"

"That is correct, my dear," she agreed, the humor reforming her two dimples. "Among ourselves, we are known as the Circle of Friends."

"Meester Jake." Ahmet was fairly dancing in place as Jake bounced up the stairs after lunch. "Is unauthorized stranger in your outer office."

"I told you not to call me that," Jake said, brushing by the little man as though he was not there. He had just spent an hour listening to Pierre moan about the barriers being placed in his way and was in no mood to pander to such whinings.

"But this man—"

Jake wheeled about, put on his sharpest parade-ground face. "Did you hear what I just said?"

Ahmet backed up a step and protested, "This most serious matter!"

"So is this," Jake said sharply. "If you want to talk with me, you will learn a proper form of address. Got that?" Before Ahmet could reply, he wheeled about and pushed through the front doors.

Corporal Samuel Bailey snapped to attention when Jake appeared. "Afternoon, Colonel."

"Don't they ever let you sleep?"

"Aye, sir." Being a graduate of Parris Island, the corporal took no notice of Jake's continual steam. "The first Tuesday of every other month."

Jake bit down on the smile as Ahmet scurried up alongside. "My new *assistant* shown up yet?"

"About an hour ago, sir." Just a flicker of a glance Ahmet's way, no more. "Mrs. Ecevit walked him up personally. She's already started the vetting process."

"That's the kind of news I like," Jake declared. "Efficiency and good news in equal measure."

A sudden thought turned him back. Ahmet missed bouncing off him by a hair. "You wouldn't know what Sergeant Adams' first name is, would you, Samuel?"

"Sergeants don't have first names, sir," Bailey replied. "They have them surgically removed when they earn their stripes."

"Morning, Daniel," Jake said, firmly shutting the door in Ahmet's protesting face. He surveyed the pile of boxes fronting the rickety metal desk and demanded, "What's all this?"

"They were here when I arrived, Mr. Burnes." Daniel Levy looked up nervously from the papers in his hand. "I'm sorry. Should it be Colonel Burnes, sir?"

"Skip the sirs for a start. You can call me Jake when

we're alone. Mr. Burnes will do when guests are around." He pointed with his chin at the papers. The bearded man was evidently very nervous. Putting their relationship swiftly onto a footing of work and results might steady things down. "Any idea what this stuff is?"

"It appears to be cost estimates from a building project. Actually, several different projects in various locations." He shuffled the papers in his hand. "But they are hopelessly jumbled. It appears that no one has made any effort whatsoever to keep note of the incoming or outgoing flow of money. The reports were simply dumped into these boxes as soon as they arrived."

"Figures." Jake glanced about the bare, seedy office. "This place could sure use some dressing up."

"I am quite comfortable, sir, I mean, Mr. Burnes."

"Mr. Burnes it is," Jake said easily. "Okay. We've got to get a few things straight. Number one, we're probably on our own here, at least in the beginning. Number two, we're going to be facing pressures from all sides. Refer all such prodders to me. Number three, I need you to get this mess straightened out as quickly as possible. Tell me where the projects are located, who the major players are in each case. See if you can get some idea what they're doing. I want to go into my first meetings with at least a basic knowledge of what is going on."

"I understand." Daniel gradually stilled, his nerves easing with the focus of a task at hand.

"Time is crucial here. The faster we can work, the greater chance we have of catching the opposition off guard."

"You can count on me, Mr. Burnes."

"I know I can," Jake said, and meant it. "Notice anything peculiar so far?"

Daniel glanced at the piles he had already sorted. "Only that there are no tender documents among these. None I have found so far, that is."

"I don't understand. My basic instructions were that each project was to be awarded after a minimum of three bids had been received, the project going to the lowest qualified bidder."

"Well, perhaps they are in the two boxes over there," Daniel said doubtfully. "I have not looked in them yet. But I started with the ones dated earliest, and so far there is nothing except requisitions for more funds and receipts for money spent."

"Then something isn't right," Jake said. "Keep digging."

"I will, Mr. Burnes." A moment's hesitation, then more quietly, "You cannot imagine what it means to receive this job."

Jake nodded, crossed his arms, said, "I have to warn you, Daniel, there is a chance that our little party here might end up being short-lived."

"Mrs. Ecevit has warned me of the obstacles we face." A different form of uncertainty surfaced, one more akin to embarrassment. "My wife, you must understand, she was overjoyed to receive this news. She has asked if you might be able to join us tonight."

Jake took in the same shiny suit as yesterday, the evident hunger, said quietly, "I don't think I could make it for dinner. But I would be delighted to stop by after for coffee."

"That would be wonderful. Thank you."

"The thanks are all on my side." Jake turned for the door. "I'm going to see the personnel people, wherever they are. I want to arrange for you to have a bonus for starting early. Say I used it as a kicker, since we needed to get going quickly. Whatever I can arrange for you to receive, I'll have them drop it by this afternoon. Then I'll be up with Mrs. Ecevit."

Jake caught a glimpse of Daniel's face as he closed the door. The look of unmasked gratitude carried him through the aggravating process of wrangling funds from a tight-fisted personnel officer. That done, he traipsed up the stairs and down the long corridor to the political officer's outer office.

He knocked on the open door, watched the sharply chiseled face rise from her papers. He asked Mrs. Ecevit, "Can you spare a few minutes?"

"I suppose so," she said reluctantly.

"Thanks." Jake entered the office, motioned to the single high-backed chair. "Mind if I sit down?"

"Please." There was no warmth to her invitation nor her eyes. She watched him with a blank stare, giving nothing away. "Mr. Edders said you wanted to ask me questions."

"That's right. I was wondering if you could give me some background on the political situation here."

The wariness did not ease. "Why?"

"So I won't have to walk in blind," Jake said simply.

She sighed. "It is not a simple Western sort of situation here, Mr. Burnes."

"Why," Jake said mildly, "does this not come as a surprise?"

She looked at him sharply, found no derision, and after a moment's hesitation said, "In the 1920s, General Ataturk wrested political power from the Ottoman monarchs and introduced a limited democracy. I say limited, because only one political party was permitted. But I must also remind you that this came after more than three thousand years of rule by absolute monarchs. It is only since the late thirties, after the general's death, that opposition parties have come into existence."

Jake leaned back, delighted with the chance to sit and learn from someone willing to teach.

"When the funds arrived from the United States, they came with orders to avoid dealing with former Nazi collaborators at all costs. This was almost impossible. There were many Nazi sympathizers within *both* parties, many of whom never said so outright. The politicians, like people throughout our society, became split, some split even within themselves. One moment they saw the Nazis as examples of the discipline necessary to stop the threat of Russia and the Communists. The next, they were terrified of what a Nazi victory might mean to our country and its future."

"Good to hear."

"You must not leap to swift conclusions, Colonel Burnes. This is not America, with its history of democracy and a foundation built upon human liberty. This is Turkey. We were ancient before your continent was even discovered. We have survived thirty centuries of dictatorship and authoritarian rule. Do you hear what I am saying? Thirty centuries. Such a legacy makes many people wary of democracy. They see it as weak. They fear that the extremists will be granted too much freedom and will use it as an opportunity to wage civil war."

"And it was these same people who backed the Nazis?"

"There you go again," she replied crossly. "Trying

to place an American-style analysis upon a truly Turkish problem."

Jake leaned back, crossed his arms. "So straighten me out, why don't you?"

Dark eyes flashed fire. "In ten minutes, you want me to explain thirty centuries of struggle and conflict?"

"You could start," Jake replied, holding to his easy tone, "by explaining why it is that you are so angry with me."

"I am not angry with you," she snapped. "I am angry with the system that has placed someone like you, with no true understanding of the crisis we face, in charge of something as crucial as these building funds."

"You could do worse," Jake responded quietly.

"I don't see how," she snapped back.

"You could be facing someone who refused to listen," Jake answered. "Or was unwilling to put up with your attitude."

Mrs. Ecevit reacted as though slapped. "My what?"

"You heard me." Jake made a message of looking at his watch. "You've used up three minutes with this tirade. That leaves seven minutes for the history lesson, or more anger. Your choice."

She gave him fifteen seconds of a smoldering stare, then, "You probably do not even remember where we were."

"You were about to tell me why it was wrong to assume that the Nazi sympathizers were the ones fearing civil war."

Perhaps it was his quiet tone, perhaps the focused way he repeated the crux of their discussion. Whatever the reason, she was forced to pause for a moment and look at him with a touch more caution, a bit less resentment. "It is wrong," she finally replied, "because there were hundreds of thousands, perhaps even millions of people, who in the moments of greatest fear thought that perhaps the Nazis represented the answer. Not the Nazis themselves, you understand, but the concept of a strong central rule. That perhaps Ataturk was wrong, perhaps the country was not ready for the freedom of democracy."

"Why not?"

"Because, Colonel Burnes, democracy requires a majority consensus. It requires most people to want democracy to *succeed*. They must follow the pattern. They must vote, they must accept the rule of the leaders, they must at least try to follow the laws. If they do not, democracy breaks down. But our own people, many of them, do not *want* democracy. They see it as a Western evil."

"The Communists?"

"They are the largest and most dangerous anti-democratic faction we now face. A few of the extreme Muslim factions feel this way as well. And here is another crucial point missed by your analysts. They hear of a few extremists condemning democracy and the West, and they say this is the opinion of *all* Muslims, of *all* Turks. They are worse than wrong. They are dangerously blind to the truth."

A knock on the door turned them both around. The adjunct Fernwhistle stuck his head in and smirked at the sight of them sitting there. "Your assistant said you might be here. The consul general wants to see you, Mr. Burnes. Now."

Jake rose to his feet and extended his hand. "I would like to come back if I may."

She inspected the hand suspiciously. "Why?"

"Because I would rather hear these things from someone who is genuinely concerned," Jake replied, "than from someone who only tells me what they think I want to hear."

Her head cocked to one side, the eyes rose to meet his, and finally she accepted his hand. "Very well, Colonel Burnes. I shall be willing to tell you what I can."

"Ah, Colonel Burnes, they found you, excellent."

"Consul General Knowles," Jake said, entering the room. He stopped short at the sight of Pierre seated beside a skinny, dark-suited stranger. Beside them sat a beaming Dimitri Kolonov. Pierre's expressive face flashed him a warning frown, then settled back into masklike stillness. Jake turned back to the consul general. "Sorry, sir, I didn't know a meeting was scheduled."

"Strictly impromptu. You know Major Servais of the French consulate, I believe. With him is the consul general's adjunct, forgive me, I have not caught your name."

"Corget, m'sieur." The man spoke without moving his lips, his face as stiff as the rest of him. His slender moustache looked painted on.

"Right. And this is Mr. Kolonov from the Russian consular staff."

"We've met."

"Indeed we have, Colonel." The Russian appeared to have an inexhaustible supply of tailored suits and fine silk ties. He exuded an ice-cold cheer as he rose to his feet and shook Jake's hand. "I would have hoped to have heard from you before now."

"Just trying to get on with my job," Jake replied.

"Which brings us to the matter of this little gathering. Sit down, Colonel. I'm afraid I have a meeting scheduled to begin in less than ten minutes, so we will need to come right to the point."

"That should not take long." The Frenchman's moustache writhed like a captured caterpillar as he spoke. "This morning I have received a strongly worded protest from the Turkish government. It appears that funds they have been expecting to receive have not yet arrived."

"I regret to report that just such a protest has arrived at my office as well," Dimitri reported apologetically.

"To my office as well, the third this week," Fernwhistle said smugly. "And the British. Their adjunct was on the phone to me this morning, wondering what the holdup was."

"That is simple enough," Jake replied. "I have not yet authorized payment."

"And why not, pray tell?" the Frenchman demanded.

"Because I need to make sure the money is being spent correctly," Jake replied. "And could somebody tell me why the Turkish government is taking such an interest in payments to local companies?"

"Because companies and the government," Dimitri replied smoothly, "are one and the same."

"Come again?" Jake looked from one face to the next. "You mean we're dealing with government-owned companies?"

"Bravo," Fernwhistle said. "I do believe he is finally catching on."

"That will do," Consul General Knowles interjected. "You see, Colonel, before the war, the Ataturk regime took on the monumental task of propelling this country from what amounted to medieval serfdom into the twentieth century. They did so by using government funds to establish modern companies in a variety of industries."

Jake looked from one man to the next. "So no alternate bidders are available for our projects?"

"None that matter," the Frenchman sniffed.

"My dear Colonel, the other companies are privately owned," Dimitri Kolonov said, false regret oozing from his voice. "And private ownership is being pushed forward by the opposition party."

"Everything is becoming clear," Jake said. "The party preferred by Russia, I take it, is the one in power."

A glint of something beneath the polished surface flashed into Kolonov's gaze. "The party in power is *everyone's* friend."

"Right." Jake turned and spoke to the group as a whole. "My orders are explicit. I am to obtain tenders from three companies for each project, then assign the project to the lowest bidder."

"Preposterous!" Fernwhistle almost bounced from his chair. "This is absolutely outrageous."

"I agree wholeheartedly with my colleague." The Frenchman's moustache threatened to crawl right off his face. "To delay payment any longer would be absurd!"

"I'm afraid our gallant ally has a point, Colonel," Kolonov purred. "There is no time for such a search. Nor would we want to offend our hosts."

"Those are my orders," Jake said, biting down hard on each word.

"Well, not for long," Fernwhistle announced with grim satisfaction. "I have just received word that a dispatch that promises to rectify this ridiculous setup once and for all is due from Washington in three days."

Tom Knowles turned a cold eye onto his assistant. "Why was I not informed of this?"

Fernwhistle gave his bow tie a nervous tug. "It just came over the wire as we were gathering for this meeting, sir."

"Well, that changes matters, then." Tom Knowles showed a weary resignation as he rose to his feet. "I suggest we postpone any further discussion until this dispatch arrives. Good day, gentlemen."

In the corridor outside the consul general's office, Dimitri Kolonov patted Jake on the back. "I would urge you to come to our reception tomorrow night, Colonel. Enjoy the splendor which your position offers you." The steely glint resurfaced. "While there is still time."

Jake walked slowly and watched the others pull away in a tight cluster, leaving him and Pierre momentarily isolated. Pierre murmured, "Three days."

"Not much time." Jake shook his head.

"We must act fast," Pierre said grimly.

"What we need," Jake agreed, "is something that points to genuine wrongdoing. I sense in my gut that corruption is rife. We've got to locate a lever that will pull the lid off this mess and expose the need for something other than political shenanigans to be in control here."

Pierre's face folded into deep furrows. "I did not know you spoke Turkish."

"What?"

"These shenanigans, they are the party in power, yes?"

Jake had to smile. "It's good to have you on my side in this."

"Yes, you do indeed need me," Pierre agreed.

"I better get back to digging," Jake said. Three days.

"On that, my hands are tied," Pierre said. "But find something, my friend, anything that needs tracking down, and then together we shall spring into action."

Jake nodded, distracted by a tiny thread of thought that came and went so fast he almost lost it. Then it returned, gathering strands.

Pierre saw it happen and declared, "You have a plan."

"Sort of."

"I know that look," Pierre insisted, and clapped his friend on the back. "Suddenly I am eager for the days to come."

Chapter Seven

Jake bounded down the stairs from the consul general's meeting, and he entered Mrs. Ecevit's office with such force that he almost startled her from her seat.

"Sorry," he said, breathless from the chance that there might truly be something to do. "Can you arrange a meeting with the opposition party?"

She settled back, but the startled expression did not leave her face. Instead, it deepened to outright consternation. "What?"

"The opposition party," Jake said, unable to contain his impatience. Three days. "And fast. I need to talk with them immediately."

"But," she glanced at her watch, "it is after four o'clock."

"Tomorrow morning, then. Early as possible."

Her impeccable English slipped a notch. "This meeting, it is most important?"

Jake let his desperation show through. "If anything has ever been urgent, it is this."

"Very well," she said carefully. As though in his demand he had uncovered something. "I can do this."

"Outstanding." He felt the tension ease a fraction.

"And could you come with me as translator? I'd be happy to clear it with your boss."

"The man I have in mind speaks excellent English," she said, finally gathering herself. "But yes, I would like to come."

"I do not like this," Jasmyn declared.

"It's too late in the afternoon to start playing tourist," Sally agreed. "But Phyllis said this tour guide might have something important."

"*Could* have information that *might* be important," Jasmyn repeated. "And we have a thousand things waiting for us to do at our new home."

Sally stopped to smile at her friend, amused but pleased at her transformation from freedom fighter and desert princess to doting bride. "You are happy being married."

Jasmyn nodded shyly. "And Pierre has been so worried. I do not like him coming back to the hotel and finding our room empty."

"He is a very lucky man," Sally said quietly.

"He has made me very happy," Jasmyn replied simply. "I want to do the same for him."

"If there is something truly important here," Sally said, "we should find it out."

Jasmyn hesitated, then decided, "Not a moment longer than necessary."

Beyond the square and the mosques stood the Topkapi Palace. From a distance, the buildings were lost within the surrounding park. Only the corner peaks rose higher than the trees, shadows of the past looming above the leafy green. Jasmyn and Sally followed the throng down the broad passage, slowed with the others at the entrance gates, and searched. Almost all the faces around them were Turkish.

Suddenly a smiling face in a blue tour-guide uniform appeared and announced, "Welcome to Topkapi. I am Jana. Come, we must hurry in order to visit the important chambers before the palace closes for the night."

As she led them through the main gates and down an ancient cobblestone lane, Jana went on, "The Topkapi Palace was home to sultans for more than six hundred years."

"I did not come here for a history lesson," Jasmyn murmured.

The guide gave no sign of hearing. "Come, we must inspect the treasury."

"I have no—"

A hand fastened upon her arm. "Come, I said."

They entered the inner courtyard, passed between the hulking guards, and entered a low-ceilinged dungeon full of museum-style display cases. Despite their impatience, the first case drew an appreciative gasp.

"Yes, there, now this is better," the young woman said quietly. "Just another pair of Western tourists viewing some of Istanbul's many treasures." When a group moved up alongside, the woman's voice became brisk. "This eighty-six carat diamond is the fifth largest in the world. And the gold sheath beyond it contains the Topkapi dagger, handled only by the ruling sultan. The largest of those three emeralds you see there at the crest is hollowed out and opens to reveal a watch inside."

Sally waited until they had moved away from the tourists, then demanded quietly, "Why are we here?"

"Look, see here, one throne after another, all covered with gold and studded with precious stones.
There is a saying that here in this one room is enough
gold to make copper seem rare."

"If we were not going to be able to talk," Jasmyn
insisted, "why did you ask us to come?"

"Because you are being followed and closely
watched," the woman said, swinging around. "Now,
please, for all our sakes, play the politely interested
tourist.

"You have to remember, of course," the woman
went on more loudly, "that a fifth of all the spoils of
war were the sultans' due. And the Ottomans won
many wars. They conquered and ruled all of Greece,
much of Eastern Europe, all of North Africa, Egypt,
and the Middle East." She pointed toward the stairs
rising from the chamber's far end. "Come, we must
visit the harem."

They allowed themselves to be led up a winding set
of steep stone stairs. Just as Sally's head rose above the
treasure vaults, she glanced back to see who if anyone
was watching her way.

"Don't turn around, that's a good dear," the woman
hummed lightly, her words swiftly lost to tight echoes
and the scraping of their shoes.

"I wonder if anyone is actually following us at all,"
Jasmyn whispered back.

The woman waited until they had reached the rise
and entered a grandly decorated chamber to say, "Let
us hope you never have to meet them face-to-face."
Then, as others crowded in behind them, she steered
them over to one corner and continued in a louder
voice, "This grand chamber was the central parlor of
the harem, the forbidden court of the imperial wives

and their children. It was guarded over by eunuchs and elder women, their lives as shrouded in mystery then as now."

Sally glanced about the lofty hall, with its rose-marble pillars, its gleaming balustrades and chandeliers and deep covering of carpets. "It looks like a gilded cage."

"And indeed it was. It was often a lonely and degrading existence, especially for those out of favor with the sultan or the senior wives. These rooms harbored intrigue and vicious conflict, the women vying to become the power behind the throne. At the peak of Ottoman rule, these chambers were home to more than a thousand women."

"So sad," Jasmyn murmured.

"Come." The guide led them down a narrow passage, showing the chambers where the women lived their quarantined existence. "The Topkapi is more than just a palace," she told them. "It was known as the Forbidden City of the Sultans, and for many of these women it was the only world they ever saw."

The rooms grew cramped and dingy as they continued down the passage toward the chambers occupied by the most junior of wives. Pressed by passing time and by other, more lustrous sights, the crowds did not follow. Jana stopped and listened for a full minute, one hand upraised to hold them to stillness.

Once she was certain they were truly alone, the professional smile fell away. "We have only a moment," she whispered. "A friend works within the Russian consulate. She has heard them speak of your husbands."

Jasmyn's voice had a catch which even the echoes

and the whispers could not erase. "They are in danger?"

"There is great concern that they are going to uncover something. What, we have not been able to determine. But whatever it is, the Russians are most concerned that it remain a secret."

"That's not much to go on," Sally murmured.

"Listen, then. The Russians have prepared a subterfuge. You have heard of the dolls called *matrioshka*?"

"The painted wooden dolls, one inside the other," Sally said. "I had one when I was a child."

"We use them to describe how the Russian mind attacks a problem," Jana said, her voice a pressing hiss. "Your husbands must not be taken in by what *appears* to be the problem. There is something else. Something deeper. Something the Russians are determined to keep hidden at all cost."

"But how—"

Footsteps scraped along the corridor. Instantly Jana straightened and became the smiling tour guide once more. "Yes, I agree, this is a most fascinating set of chambers. But, please follow me, there is so much more to see, and so little time."

Daniel Levy rushed over as Jake climbed from the taxi. "It is so good of you to come, Mr. Burnes."

"My pleasure." Jake tried to shake off the distraction of having found neither Sally nor a note when he had returned to their hotel. He had shrugged off his disappointment with the thought that she and Jasmyn were probably working at the apartment, where they were scheduled to move in two days. If, Jake amended

his thoughts, they were not moved out of Turkey entirely by that time. He glanced up at the crumbling
building that fronted the noisy street and asked Daniel
Levy, "You live here?"

"No, no, but this is as far as a taxi will bring you,
and you could never find your way alone the first time.
Please come." He led Jake through what at first appeared to be a side entrance to the half-ruined structure but in fact proved to be a long, narrow passage. "I
regret to inform you, Mr. Burnes, that my father has
decided to join us tonight."

"It will be nice to meet him."

Daniel Levy cast a doubtful glance back over his
shoulder. "I am afraid that might not be true. My father
has strong feelings against, well, against foreigners."

"You mean," Jake interpreted, "he doesn't much
care for non-Jews. Given what he's recently gone
through, I can't say I blame him."

"He is old, and he has been sick. For some time he
has lived for little more than the synagogue, the Torah,
and we his family." Daniel turned down another lane,
the balconies overhead almost touching across the passage. "Age requires that we grant allowances that otherwise would not be permitted."

"He wishes you were working for a Jewish company," Jake guessed. "He wants to size up the opposition, see if he can scare them off."

Daniel sighed to a stop at a tiny intersection. "You
are a most observant man, Mr. Burnes."

"Don't worry," Jake assured him. "I've been given
lots of practice recently at keeping hold of my temper."

"This is not," Daniel said quietly, "how I had hoped
the evening would proceed."

"Then we'll just have to make it the first of many,"

Jake said, and glanced down the side passages. Both led off in winding mystery. "What is this place?"

"One of the ancient Christian quarters," he explained, glanced at his watch, and hurried on through the winding maze with easy familiarity. "The Muslims did not seek to cast out all their forebears. Quite the contrary. They needed them and invited many to stay. But as second-class citizens, never to rule again."

Jake looked up at the statue of a praying angel guarding a corner, so worn by time and sun and rain that the face was almost gone. This weathering granted the statue an even greater sense of gentle peace, of endless repose. "And the Jews?"

"There were a few here before, of course. The Diaspora sent Jews to settle almost everywhere they were welcome, and some places they were not." He turned into a lane more narrow than the others. None bore markings or street signs or indications of where they might lead. "But a great number fled here from Spain. You have heard of the great battles against the Moors?"

"Yes."

"The Spanish should not be condemned too harshly for their persecutions afterward." He cast a rapid smile over his shoulder. "A strange thing to hear a Jew say, but true nonetheless. The Spanish had fought for two centuries to cast out the Muslim invaders who had swept up from Africa. Many Jews followed along in the Arabs' wake, my family among them. When the Muslims were finally cast out, Spain continued in what they saw as a natural part of this same war and ordered all who remained in the country to either become Christian, or leave, or die."

"And your family came here?"

The dark beard nodded. "Once the Ottomans had

conquered Constantinople and changed its name to Istanbul, the sultans wanted to see it continue as a great trading center. But the Islamic code forbade the charging of interest, which is a necessary part of international trade. The great Ottoman families saw only two professions as fitting and proper, so their offspring either became landowners or members of the royal court. Thus the Jews and those Christians willing to remain and work under Muslim rule were invited to work as traders. More Jews than Christians accepted the invitation, for the simple reason that my ancestors had nowhere else to go."

"Your story is like a bit of living history."

"More than you might imagine. When we are alone, my family still speak the language called Ladino, the Spanish we brought with us four hundred years ago. From what we understand, this is the only place on earth where it is found today. Yet for us it still lives and breathes, a vibrant language. We have numerous books published each year, only available in our Ladino tongue." He pointed through an ancient portico. "Through here, please."

Suddenly they were enveloped by birdsong and the sweet scents of flowers and water and grass. The garden was walled and tiny, not twenty paces to a side, but coming as it did in the middle of the high-walled lanes, it was a delight. "Beautiful."

"This garden is entrance to the Jewish quarter." Daniel pointed to an ancient structure rising from one corner. "This is one of the oldest synagogues in Istanbul. My family has worshiped here for over four hundred years." They slowed their pace to enjoy the garden's radiance. "My family prospered under the Ottomans. Istanbul of the Middle Ages was both bank and warehouse for East-West trade. Letters and goods arrived from all over the world, destined for the merchant families."

He pushed through a heavy wooden gate, walked up a passage lined by a profusion of flowers, and entered an apartment building. The inner corridor was old but spotless, and smelled of cooking and disinfectant. They climbed two floors, past the sounds of children and adults and music and laughter, and stopped before a massive, age-stained door.

Daniel paused to kiss his fingers and press them against a small metal box nailed to the doorpost. He tapped lightly, opened the door, and called, "Miriam?" He then gestured to Jake. "Please, Mr. Burnes, you are welcome."

A dark-haired beauty entered the hallway, wiping her hands upon an apron. Her smile was as warm as her voice. "It is indeed an honor, Mr. Burnes."

Before Jake could respond, Daniel said quietly, "And this is my father."

Miriam's eyes dropped with her smile as an old man shuffled past her, peering at Jake with rheumy eyes. Gray curls poked from about his skullcap. When no hand was offered him, Jake gave a stiff bow and said, "An honor, Mr. Levy."

The man inspected him from head to foot, then turned to his son and demanded, "You are certain this is necessary, permitting entry to a goy?"

"Papa," Miriam said tiredly.

The old man went on to Jake, "I say this in English so that you can hear and understand, *Colonel* Burnes. Yes, yes, I know, you now hold a civilian position, but an officer is an officer is an officer. A goy and an officer of a foreign army. Here. In my house."

"Papa, please," Daniel's voice implored quietly. "You shame me."

"No, it is you who shames this house. Such an invitation, never have I heard of such a thing."

Jake kept his tone as steady as his gaze. "It is true I remain an officer in my country's army," he agreed quietly. "This is something I remain very proud of. I was called, and I served."

"America has long been friend to the Jews," Miriam said, her tone downcast.

"Yes, yes, I know of your family's sentiments," the old man snapped. "And how even now they wish for this man to come and visit them, so that they might press him for visas." He stared balefully up at Jake. "But my place is here, I tell you. This has been home to my family for almost five hunared years. Twice again as long as America has been a nation."

"He has been ill," Daniel said apologetically.

"I am not ill," the old man retorted. "I am confident in the face of my adversaries."

"Papa, shame. He is a friend."

" 'Though an host should encamp against me,' " Jake quoted, wanting only peace with the old man, admiring him and his stubborn strength, " 'my heart shall not fear: though war should rise against me, in this will I be confident.' "

"What is this?" The old man backed up a pace in astonishment. "You are quoting the Psalms to me?"

"Did I not say?" Daniel spoke quietly. "An exceptional man, Papa."

"Please, please, you must enter," Miriam urged, ushering Jake down the hall and into the living room. "Take this seat here. It is the most comfortable. Daniel, come help me in the kitchen, please. Papa, you must behave, do you hear?"

Jake remained standing, looking around the room. It was cluttered with the possessions of ages—chairs etched with ancient floral patterns, a high-backed wooden bench scrolled with Hebraic writing, a copper-topped central table, aged carpets upon the floor. Jake found himself drawn to a series of framed prints upon the walls. Most were in Hebrew, but one was in a different, almost cuneiform-shaped script.

"My ancestor received that letter some two hundred years ago. It is curious that you would choose it to inspect." The old man watched Jake from his chair. "You see, Colonel, that letter is from a Christian, one you would probably call a soldier, but we would prefer to think of as a pirate. Of course, what are we but ignorant Jews?"

"I would never have thought of you in such a way," Jake said, taking the chair Miriam had shown him.

But the old man did not let up. "That letter, Colonel Burnes, was written by this Christian *pirate*, who had captured an ancestor of mine and was allowing him to send one letter begging for ransom money. The Christian, you see, was willing to sell this innocent trader and his family for the price of one sack of gold per family member. The trader was begging for his life." The old man's gaze was bright and keen and watchful. "My family has kept that letter upon our wall ever since as both reminder and warning to watch out against the treachery of outsiders."

"It was not Christians who imprisoned you and your son in the camp," Jake pointed out.

"No, indeed not." The dark eyes remained steady and accusing. "Not this time."

"Enough of this, enough." Daniel entered the room bearing a platter of sweets. "We did not invite this man into our home to insult him."

But Jake kept his eye upon the old man, held by a sudden thought so strong he knew it was a gift, an invitation. "I wonder," he said calmly, "if there might not be a point where we can know a meeting of the minds."

"Impossible," the old man expostulated.

"Perhaps a meeting of the hearts as well," Jake went on, feeling the gentle guiding force. "Perhaps even, in time, become friends."

The old man's eyes narrowed, but something held him silent. Daniel stood over the pair of them, his questioning gaze shifting back and forth.

Jake leaned forward. "I would consider it an honor," he said quietly, "if you would teach me of the Torah."

Chapter Eight

J ake sighed his way into the office building's ancient elevator. He watched as Mrs. Ecevit slid the brass accordion doors shut and pressed the top-floor button. He waited as the floors clanked by, his mind far too slack for what lay ahead. But he could not help it. His world was out of kilter. His heart thudded miserably in his chest. He sighed again.

Mrs. Ecevit glanced his way. "There is something wrong?"

He started to deny it but did not have the strength. "I argued with my wife. Last night. And again this morning."

"Ah." She nodded. "Men are such bad quarrelers."

"*I* sure am." Jake watched her ratchet the inner door back and push the outer one open, then followed her out. "I can't win a debate. She's much more intelligent than I am. So I lose my temper and end up ordering her to do what I want her to do."

For the very first time a hint of something human, something warm and compassionate, showed through Mrs. Ecevit's brittle shell. She slowed her pace. "I do not know American women, but if they are anything like intelligent Turkish women, they would not like such an order very much."

"No," Jake agreed. "Sally sure doesn't."

He tried to compose himself as they entered a large outer office, but the weight of his heart pulled his face back into the same slack lines. Jake watched from the doorway as she walked over and gave their names to an attractive receptionist.

Mrs. Ecevit returned to where he stood and said, "We are early, and the man we are scheduled to meet has other people with him."

"No problem." Jake sank down into the corner seat, as removed as possible from the cheerful bustle filling the large chamber. Mrs. Ecevit took the seat beside him, her eyes darkly humorous. He said, "I'd give anything never to have to argue with her, not ever again."

The humor broke through then, and Mrs. Ecevit dropped ten years as she flashed white teeth and chuckled. "Ah, Mr. Burnes, you Americans are so wonderful at times."

"Call me Jake. I can't be talking about something this personal and hear you call me by my last name."

"All right." Another flashing smile, and he realized that beneath that diamond-hard exterior dwelled a truly striking woman. "You may call me Anya. There is an expression we use very often, 'Tomorrow, tomorrow the apricots.' It is very Turkish. The story goes, once there was a handsome young man, just like yourself, I imagine. He was pressing his favors upon a lovely young maiden. As he grew more impatient for her answer, she replied, yes, all right, but tomorrow, tomorrow when the apricots appear on that tree. Only the tree she was pointing to was a pear tree."

"Meaning I'm asking for the impossible."

"Yes," she agreed, trying to recover her accustomed solemnness, but the light in her eyes giving her away. "But it is very nice that you would even wish for such a thing. It is very romantic. Would it be impertinent of me to ask what happened?"

Jake sighed his way into the tale, the situation he faced becoming impossibly entangled with his worry—Sally's meeting the two women on the train, the Russian's appearance, the confrontation with Fernwhistle, Sally and Jasmyn's talk with Mrs. Hollamby, his own meeting yesterday afternoon with the consul general and the time limit placed on him. "Then when I came home last night," he went on, "Sally had just arrived back from some clandestine meeting at a place called Topeppy."

"Topkapi," Anya corrected. "The sultans' summer palace."

"Whatever you say. Anyway, she and Jasmyn were led around by a stranger who tells them the Russians have planned some deception to pull us off the track."

"It would not surprise me," Anya said slowly. "That would be very much a Soviet-type strategy."

"This woman also told her we were being followed. All of us. Then they heard something and hightailed it away." Jake grimaced at the thought. "I was furious that she'd taken such a risk."

"And she," Anya finished for him, "was furious that you did not appreciate her efforts."

"Don't tell me you were in the lobby and heard us." He dropped his head. "I can't believe we argued in a hotel. We might as well have been standing in the middle of the street."

"Hotel staffs are paid to be discreet. And no, I was not there, I did not need to be. It is one of the most ancient of disagreements. You want to protect her, she wants to help you."

Jake lifted his head. "So what's the answer?"

"For you to be grateful, and for her to be careful." Again the flashing smile. "And keep hoping that the tree will someday grow apricots."

"Anya, so sorry to have kept you waiting." A young man in a finely cut Western suit rushed over, took both Anya's hands in his, smiled, then turned as Jake rose to his feet and offered his hand. "And you must be Colonel Burnes."

"This is my husband, Turgay Ecevit," Anya said.

"Your husband," Jake said dully.

"Turgay is director of this office, which runs the party's Istanbul-based operations," she said with quiet pride. "He is also personal assistant to Celal Bayar, leader of the Turkish opposition." She looked up at her husband, then back at Jake. "As you can see, I did not need to hear your discussion of last night. I know it all too well."

Her husband looked from one to the other. "What is this?"

"Just finishing a discussion," she said quietly. "Perhaps we should begin another. Colonel Burnes has very little time."

Istanbul was a world of endless contrasts, where modern met the ancient and the timeless held place with the immediate. Handcarts bustled between smoky buses and clanging streetcars. Donkeys brayed as they pulled wooden carts and impossible loads. Women stepped over craters in the sidewalks, one hand gripping eager children while the other fanned the flames of conversation. Great clouds of noise and diesel fumes and fresh energy billowed in the air. Despite the ache she felt over quarreling with Jake, Sally found herself captivated by the excitement and the mystery of it all.

The fish market was on the legendary stretch of water known as the Golden Horn, an inlet of the Bosphorus. The stalls did not line the streets because there was simply no room. The buildings bellied right up to the street, and the lane dropped directly into the rock-lined water. Enterprising fishermen used broad flat-bottomed boats as stalls, standing in one end, calling their endless song of quality and selection and price and barter, one hand slinging water over the stock to keep it shining and fresh. Potential customers walked the crowded lane, leaned over the railing, waved their arms, and argued prices with exuberance. Overhead, gulls echoed their boisterous refrain.

"Ah, there you are, my dear. And on time yet again. How marvelous." Phyllis Hollamby walked up, moving briskly even while leaning heavily on her cane. "And where is your lovely companion?"

"She had to attend another reception with her husband."

"Pity. But it can't be helped, I suppose." A keen ear picked up on the unsaid. "What did your husband think of the information you got from Jana?"

"I'm not sure," Sally said dismally. "We ended up arguing about my taking risks."

Phyllis gave a magnificent sniff. "Men. They are so utterly blind at times, aren't they, my dear?"

"Jake is a wonderful man," Sally said defensively.

"No doubt, no doubt. And he must love you dearly,

to have such concern for your well-being. Yet one would think that, given the critical nature of his affairs, he would welcome a bit of help."

"Not to mention the time pressure," Sally added, and related the three-day ultimatum.

"Well, there you are." The dimples appeared in age-spotted cheeks. "Still, I suppose if men did ever reach perfection, life would become an utter bore. Don't you agree?"

Despite the weight of her heart, Sally could not help but smile in reply. "I don't think there's much chance of that."

"That's my girl." Mrs. Hollamby reached over and patted Sally's cheek. "Your husband is a most fortunate gentleman. I hope he realizes that."

"He does," she said, then amended, "most of the time."

"Well, we shall just have to remind him, then, won't we?" She spun about. "Come along, my dear. I smell adventure on the wind."

Sally hung back. "Jake doesn't want me taking any more risks."

"Who said anything about risks?" Phyllis sniffed. "From now on, we shall limit ourselves strictly to a bit of sightseeing. Not even your gallant but somewhat overprotective husband can object to that."

"Have you heard, Colonel, of *yagli güres*?"

Jake accepted a tulip-shaped tea glass from the attendant, holding it gingerly by the rim. "I don't even know if it's animal, vegetable, or mineral."

"None of them." Turgay accepted his glass, thanked

the young man, sipped noisily. "It is a distinctly Turkish form of wrestling in which men oil down their bodies, then grapple for a hold to throw their opponent off
his feet. It is a dance of conflict and balance and opposing powers, and it says much about my land. We
grapple with ourselves, Colonel. The modern with the
ancient, the Muslim with the secular, the democratic
with the authoritarian, the internal with the great powers to every side. To govern Turkey is a constant struggle in which one slip spells disaster."

Jake lifted his glass, felt the liquid's near-boiling
heat before his lips touched the rim, lowered it without
tasting. Drinking such tea had to be an acquired trait.
"Sounds like a risky business to be in."

"To understand just how risky, Colonel, it is necessary to explain a bit of our history." A more thoughtful sip, then, "In 1453, after a bombardment lasting
fifty days, the city fell to the Ottoman Turks. It is said
that the paintings and mosaics upon the church walls
sweated from fear. The pope himself offered daily
prayers for deliverance from what he saw as two
equally great evils, a large comet and the Ottoman
ruler, Sultan Mehmet. But the city did fall to the sultan.
The city of Constantinople was renamed Istanbul, and
a period of Ottoman domination began which lasted
almost exactly five hundred years. The domination
was absolute. Opposition to the ruling sultan and his
court was strictly forbidden. There was only one voice,
one law. And with time, this law became increasingly
corrupt. By the time World War One broke out and the
sultan decided to side with the Germans, Turkey was
trapped within the nightmare of a hopelessly back-
ward, hopelessly corrupt regime. Time and the rest of
the world had passed us by."

Turgay had more the air of a passionate professor than a politician. He was tall and striking, with chiseled olive features and intelligent eyes. He carried his authority with the ease of one for whom such trappings mattered little. The fire of conviction ignited both his gaze and his words. "After the debacle of World War One, a general called Mustafa Kemal, later renamed Ataturk, which means Father of the Turks, led a war of insurrection against the corrupt Ottoman rule. The struggle ended in 1923. In the eyes of the common man, Ataturk had won a victory on par with Mehmet's original taking of Constantinople. This gave him the power to sweep aside Ottoman history and declare Turkey a republic.

"Ataturk was determined to drag Turkey out of the Middle Ages and into the twentieth century. To him, this meant a complete break with the Ottoman religious past. So Turkey became not only a republic, but also secular, meaning that religion and state were separated once and for all. Ataturk also embarked on a rapid expansion of state enterprise, education, and health care. The Latin alphabet replaced the Arabic, and the entire nation, literally, went to school. For the first time in its history, the common man was given the opportunity to read and write. And women were freed from imprisonment behind the *sharia*, or Islamic code of law."

Anya Ecevit sat listening to the history lesson with a patience that surprised Jake, seemingly content to set aside her normal drive and energy and share in her husband's interest. Jake found himself watching her as much as Turgay. "Yet there was a downside, as you Americans say, to this reform," Turgay went on. "A very great one. All these new laws were strictly enforced. No opposition, or even opposing thought, was permitted. Anyone who voiced an opinion contrary to the new, modern, secular state was considered a traitor."

"Sounds familiar."

"Indeed, yes. Fortunately for Turkey, Ataturk was both a charismatic leader and a statesman, a figure greater than life, one determined to lead Turkey not toward aggression, but rather toward a new future."

"You sound almost awed when you talk of him," Jake said. "Strange to hear, coming from an opposition politician."

"In your country, perhaps. But in my country, Ataturk was in truth the *only* politician. It is because of him that we are free to be politicians at all. So you see, Mr. Burnes, although I disagree with where the country has arrived, I do not disagree with the path upon which it trod nor the leader who brought us here."

"This Ataturk must have been quite a man."

"Indeed he was." He grimaced apologetically. "But Turkish politics remain treacherous, Colonel, with intrigue and corruption practiced with a skill learned over hundreds of years. That is what we the opposition are up against when we begin speaking of much-needed change."

Jake decided his tea had cooled enough to risk a sip. "So what is the answer?"

"We of the Democratic Party do not condemn Ataturk's policies. Our leader was himself once a prime minister under Ataturk. But we feel that if progress is going to continue, private enterprise must be given a chance to succeed. We are worried that if both political power and business remain within the hands of central government, the old problems of corruption and intrigue will resurface."

"And strangle you all over again," Jake agreed. "I don't see why there hasn't been American support for this."

The couple exchanged glances before Turgay responded quietly, "Nor do we, Colonel. Especially after we won almost a third of the parliamentary seats in the last election. But your government persists in seeing any opposition as a threat to stability and an entry point for the Communists. We have been trying to tell them that unless we are given an equal chance to express our views, in other words, be the opposition in the truest sense of the word, the risk of Communist revolt is even stronger. But it has been hard to find someone willing to hear us out. So very hard."

"I have been trying to set up a meeting like this one," Anya added, "for almost a year."

"People are too busy, there is too much going on, they are worried about rocking the boat," Turgay said. "We understand some of the reasons. But we disagree as well."

"So do I," Jake agreed. "I don't know if I can help, especially as I might be replaced in a matter of days. But maybe, just maybe, we can set some wheels in motion."

"This is the chance I have been searching for," Turgay exclaimed, leaning forward in his seat. "Tell us what we need to do."

The ferry from Istanbul to the Asian shore was a welcome release from the city's fierce grip. "Istanbul is one of the most marvelous cities in the world," Phyllis declared fondly. "It straddles Europe and Asia and joins the cultures of East and West. Not to mention the wealth of its past. So much history, so many civilizations, that time blurs, and the city comes to count the years as mortal man does minutes."

She pointed toward the approaching shore. "The lands that lie in Asia are known as Anatolia. Some of the local villagers declare themselves citizens of Anatolia, not Turkey. They are a fiercely patriotic lot."

Sally gazed across the azure waters to the gently sloping hills. "This is beautiful."

"There is talk of a bridge, but many are against it. I most certainly count myself among them. It would only mean more hurry and rush, and the city already has far too much of both." She took a deeply satisfied breath of the sea breeze. "Crossing the Bosphorus by bridge would be like holding hands with gloves on. The thrill would simply be lost."

The city rising from the opposite shore had the look and feel of a sprawling village. The pace was slower, the air stiller, the buildings seedier, the people from a different age. Sally walked alongside the older woman and relished the delight of discovery.

They passed a shop filled with vast piles of clutter. Outside, two men sat at a rickety table, the younger man listening eagerly to the elder's lecture. Despite the heat, the old man wore a blue knit skullcap in the manner of one who seldom if ever took it off. Sprouting from either side was a flowing white beard that fell broad and square to cover the top three buttons of his tattered shirt. One hand curled around his cane, while the other directed the flow of conversation in the air between him and his younger companion.

"My husband operated one of the largest foreign-owned companies in Turkey," Phyllis said as they walked, her tone as casual as though she were discussing the weather. "In a land such as this, it is utterly impossible to disengage something of that size from the realm of politics and intrigue, so he inevitably found himself in the midst of things. He was as adamantly opposed to my own involvement as your husband is to yours. But in time he came to see me as an invaluable asset, able to hear things and visit places utterly closed to him." She gave Sally a reassuring smile. "You must give him time, my dear. It is not true that men don't change. They do, but ever so slowly."

A hint of the previous evening's frustration resurfaced. "I'd rather watch a glacier melt."

The dimples reappeared. "You do my heart such good, my dear. If you will permit an ancient woman's advice, perhaps you need to learn patience to match your own husband's need for greater open-mindedness."

They stopped to permit passage to a young man in khaki overalls carrying a stack of empty oil cans. His load rose up to a level twice his height. A coiled blanket draped over his shoulders granted some padding to his back. The ropes that tied his load were tangled into one great knot, which he gripped with both hands. He huffed noisily with each step.

The sight of the young man laboring like a pack horse sobered Phyllis. When he had passed, she said, "This is a country where the present is tangled with the past. For the rich, there are the pleasures of living where the cultures of Arabia are married to the lifestyle of the Mediterranean. For the poor, I am sorry to say, the life of serfdom still remains."

They took a cobblestone lane up between two buildings that appeared to be carved from the hillside. Despite her age, Phyllis maintained a brisk pace. Finally they stopped before an ancient house of wood and brick. It leaned tiredly upon its neighbor, the windows and doors and floors reset to remain more or less level. Phyllis raised her cane and rapped sharply on the doorframe. An older woman appeared in the entrance, as broad as she was tall, her head covered in a white scarf as translucent as a veil. She beamed toothlessly at the sight of Phyllis, backed up with as much a bow as she could manage, and invited them in.

"It is polite to take off your shoes here," Phyllis said quietly. The woman offered them pairs of house slippers decorated with brightly colored beads and hand-sewn designs, then led them through the foyer and into her home.

The floors were of broad wooden planking, darkened with centuries of oil and polish. The carpets were gay, even those so worn that the designs had become mere grayish shadows. The living room table was broad and low and circular, and carved from a single sheet of bronze. An old man rose from a low divan and tottered over, hand outstretched. Phyllis greeted him with a genuine smile and words in Turkish. Sally allowed herself to be directed toward a padded couch standing barely a foot above the floor. She followed Phyllis's example and half sat, half knelt with her skirt tucked tightly around her knees.

Phyllis turned to her and said, "This gentleman used to be employed by my husband's company. You will find that in these lands, such employment creates the sense of an extended family, with all the obligations and duties of a patriarch."

The old woman returned with a copper tray bearing four ceramic cups, each nestled within its own copper shell, and an oddly shaped long-handled vase. Instantly the room was filled with the fragrance of coriander and coffee. Sally said to Phyllis, "I didn't know you spoke Turkish."

"Only a few words," she replied modestly before returning to an animated discussion with the old man. The woman left once more and returned with a second tray, which she set down between Phyllis and Sally. It appeared to be filled with unbaked dumplings, each rolled in finely sifted flour. She then lifted the bronze pitcher and poured what to Sally looked like steaming black mud into each little cup. Sally accepted her cup with murmured thanks and looked doubtfully into the tarry depths. "I'm supposed to drink this?"

"Let the sediment settle a little first," Phyllis replied brightly. "And you must take one of these Turkish delights. They are homemade."

Sally looked at the tray again and realized, "They are coated with pure sugar."

Phyllis selected one, took a bite, hummed her appreciation to the beaming old couple. "Be sure and smile when you swallow."

Sally chose the smallest and forced herself to ignore the sugar dust that filtered into her mouth and nose as she raised it and bit. The glutinous mass melted to release the highest concentration of oversweetness she had ever experienced. She swallowed it as she would medicine, forced down the choking sensation, managed, "Absolutely amazing."

"That's a dear," Phyllis said, her eyes sparkling. "I do wish you could see your face just now."

Sally held grimly to her smile, lifted the cup, swal-

lowed a mixture of fiery pungent coffee and grit. After
the sweet, the coffee was not half bad.

"Now finish the sweet," Phyllis instructed.

Sally switched her forced smile toward the English-
woman. "You've got to be joking."

"Eyes are upon you, my dear." Phyllis finished her
own, then licked her fingers in an ecstasy of appreciation. Sally watched her with astonishment, then without thinking what she was actually doing to her stom-
ach, placed the remaining candy in her mouth and took
it like an oversized pill. Phyllis smiled in approval.
"Oh, well done."

"I am about to keel over with sugar shock," Sally
said brightly to the old couple.

Phyllis laughed gaily and said something in Turkish. The couple beamed with delight and responded
animatedly. Phyllis bowed her thanks and said, "They
have just made to you a gift of all the remaining can-
dies."

"I am absolutely speechless," Sally said, bowing in
turn.

The discussion then took a somber turn, and the
elderly couple spoke at length before permitting Phyllis time to turn and translate, "They have a son who is
now working on a construction project some eighty
miles from here." She glanced at the couple, murmured, "It is most curious."

"What is?"

"Well, they say that all the men there know that the
project is funded by the Americans. But what they
would want with a cultural center built miles from
anywhere is baffling."

"Maybe they have it wrong."

"They positively insist that these two items are correct, that it is to be a cultural center, and that it is being financed by the Americans." Phyllis's normally cheerful demeanor was sobered by what she had heard. "But there is more. They say their son and all the other men are receiving two weekly payments. One is to do the construction, the other is to do it as slowly as possible."

"That," Sally decided, "makes no sense at all."

"Quite. And yet they insist it is true. And they insist there is a rumor, well, actually more than a rumor, that this second payment is quietly coming from the Russians."

Chapter Nine

H e wants to know," Daniel Levy translated for Jake, "when the next installment is going to arrive."

"Tell him the same thing I said when he asked me five minutes ago," Jake replied stubbornly. "When I've been satisfied that the first funds have been well spent."

They were seated in a tumbledown shanty propped next to a rubble-strewn pit on the outskirts of Istanbul. The documentation in Jake's file had proclaimed that this was to become part of a new factory for the production of electronic components. All Jake could see for the money spent so far was a huge hole in the ground. He turned to Daniel. "Show them the bill for the steel."

Two men sat on the other side of the desk. One was dark and short and angry, his round face covered with stubble and sweat, his hands grimy and strong. The other was slender and nervous and a talker, filling the air with words that Daniel translated in swatches of nonsense. The young man accepted the sheet only reluctantly, barely glanced at the figures to which Daniel pointed, then continued with his dialogue: They had assumed there was an understanding with the American authorities. These delays in receiving payment were slowing down the construction process. Over and over, the same words, leaving nothing answered or resolved.

Jake pointed at the bill which the man now held and said through Daniel, "That says my government has paid for seventeen tons of support girders. Where are they?"

The man's voice was a constant irritating drone. They are ordered, they are ordered, they are coming, it is all according to plan, yes, it is most unfortunate that the American gentleman does not have experience with Turkish building methods, but we are a poor country and payments must be made in advance. On and on and on the words poured from the nervous man, politely pressing for the release of funds, promising that everything was moving according to a schedule neither man could produce. All the while, his companion sat and smoldered and glared at Jake. Jake returned the stare as calmly as he could manage, feeling as though his brain were being turned to oatmeal by the endless verbiage, knowing they were intent on wearing him down.

Jake rose, knowing this was the only way to stop the noise. "I will release more funds when the girders have been delivered and when the concrete foundation, which my records show we have also already paid for, has been laid."

The burly man spoke for the first time, his words gnashed between grinding teeth. Daniel translated quietly, his calm murmur untouched by neither fatigue nor the others' rising unease. "Delay any further, and all work will stop."

"I don't see work being done anyway," Jake retorted, not fazed in the least by the man's ire. He would far prefer a battle with the builder than this endless tirade from the bureaucrat. A sudden thought caused him to ask the suited gentleman, "Are you from the government or from the construction company?"

The nervousness increased, the stream of words quickened. Before Daniel could translate, Jake held up his hand. "One word will do. We're going to start getting some straight answers around here, or I am pulling out of this mess entirely." When Daniel hesitated before translating, Jake glanced his way and said, "Tell them that word for word."

The atmosphere within the shanty instantly electrified when the words had been said. The burly man rose to his feet, shouting and gesticulating. The nervous man poured out a continual battering of words. Jake motioned with his chin for Daniel to stand. "I've had my fill. We're going to see some real work done, and we're going to start getting straight answers, or we're shutting you down." Daniel had to raise his voice to be heard. When the translation was completed, Jake ignored the response. He finished, "And that is final."

When they were back in the consular car, Jake said, "You can't tell me that what we saw there is normal progress, even for here."

"Construction materials are in short supply, so partial payment in advance could be argued for." Daniel mulled it over, then decided, "But no, what they have done so far does not explain the urgent need for more funds. And their attitude is a mystery."

"Totally baffling," Jake agreed.

"It is as if they were intentionally trying to slow us down."

Jake stared at the bearded man. "What makes you say that?"

"One would expect those who are faced with having their funds discontinued at least to offer something definite to ease the tension. A written time plan, a bit of progress, a willingness to meet you halfway." Daniel added apologetically, "Perhaps they know of your own dilemma and think they can outlast you. But if so, why did they not simply refuse to meet with you? I have the feeling that something else is at work here."

"As though they wanted to tie us up in knots," Jake suggested, "so we wouldn't look anywhere else."

Daniel considered this, his eyes never leaving Jake's face. "You have heard something?"

"My wife did." Swiftly he related what Sally had told him about the matrioshka dolls and the tour guide's warning.

"Perhaps this is indeed confirmation of her rumor." Daniel stroked his beard, said distractedly, "Your wife must be a remarkable woman."

"Yes, she is," Jake said, and felt a renewed pang over their argument. He changed the subject with, "If anyone asks, I want you to appear to be working strictly on this one project. But in truth I want you to set this aside and look for something else." Jake ran back over the discussion and shook his head. "That project was a mess, but it's not enough to keep the ax from falling on my assignment."

"You think there are watchers within the consulate?"

"Watchers, definitely. Whether or not they're actually working for the other side, I can't say. But with the pressure we're under, it's a risk we can't afford to take."

"Let me see if I understand this correctly," Pierre said, picking his way over the uneven cobblestones. "We are going to spend our evening with a man who does not like us, studying a religion that is not ours, learning from someone who does not want to teach."

Jake stopped to face his friend. "Are you about finished?"

"Forgive me, my friend. I am French. You must use your more sensible American mind to explain how I have this wrong."

"In the first place, how can he dislike you if he's never met you?"

"An excellent question," Pierre replied somberly. "I must ask him that myself."

"In the second, the Torah is the Jewish term for the Books of Moses, the first five Books of the Bible. *Our* Bible. Theirs and ours."

"I am beginning to see the light."

"Ever since I started studying the Old Testament," Jake went on, "I've wondered how the Jews see this book, which was given to them by God. Given to *them*. They had the Old Testament Scriptures in their possession for over a thousand years before Christ brought the answer to the entire world. They were the first crucible, Pierre. They were the ones who showed that the law alone was not enough."

"I believe I know you as well as anyone, save your wonderful wife," Pierre murmured. "Yet still you manage to surprise me at the unseen turn."

"This is a great opportunity," Jake persisted.

Pierre grasped Jake's arm and turned them about. "Then come, my friend. Let us go and continue with the adventure of learning."

Jake had returned from work to find Sally still out, her succinct note saying only that she had gone for some sightseeing and shopping. He had pushed aside his disappointment at not being able to apologize in person and tried as best he could to do it in a note. He had then found Pierre in the lobby, sulking over the continued frustration of being trapped within a meaningless cycle of functions and events. Jasmyn, he had reported dejectedly, was at a tea party given by the consul general's wife. Jake had taken pity on his friend and invited him along to his study time with Daniel Levy's father.

After making their way down a confusing maze of lanes, Jake was enormously pleased when the familiar little gate came into view. They crossed the synagogue's tiny garden, entered the apartment building, and climbed to the floor above Daniel's.

They were met at the top of the stairs by a suspicious gaze and a pair of skullcaps. The hand thrust forward, and the querulous voice demanded, "You must both wear the yarmulke to study Torah."

"Fine," Jake said, accepting them both. "This is my friend Pierre Servais. Pierre, this is Joseph Levy."

"I am charmed, m'sieur."

The gaze squinted down further, and the old man demanded something in French.

"I do indeed have the honor of being French," Pierre replied in English.

Again there was the rapid thrust of snappish French.

"I am here because this gentleman has brought me," Pierre replied, persisting with his English. "I am with this gentleman because he is both my friend and my teacher. That I have found to be the rarest of combinations."

The old man turned to Jake. "You speak no French?"

"Unfortunately not."

He sniffed and turned his attention back to Pierre. "Teacher of what?"

"Of all that is most important," Pierre replied solemnly. "Of all that would have remained invisible and unseen, were it not for Jake."

The response unsettled the old man. He opened the door, stepped back, and motioned for them to enter. They followed him down the entrance hall to a study filled with overstuffed horsehair furniture. "Sit, sit. I shall fetch tea."

"That is not necessary," Jake said, choosing a chair as large as a throne and slipping on the silk cap.

"Sit, I said. The water is already boiled."

Soon enough he returned, bearing a large silver tray with three glasses and a vast, ancient tome. Only after he had set down the tray did he happen to notice the books in their laps. "What are those?"

"Bibles."

"*Christian* Bibles," he said, with a great sigh and a shake of his head. Still, he handed out the glasses, then seated himself across the low table from them. He sipped his glass, making the inblown breath to cool as he drank, again, his eyes casting back and forth from one man to the other. "You have heard of the *Me Am Lo'ez*? No, of course not. How could you?"

Another sip, then he set his tea aside, and with it

his indecision. Jake actually saw it happen. As though the argument that had clouded his voice and his gaze since the earlier meeting was now over. A decision had been reached.

"Some call this the greatest work of Ladino literature ever written," Joseph Levy said, looking down upon the leather-bound volume. "Its history is the history of my people, the Jews of the Mediterranean." He swiveled that great book around so that it faced his visitors. "My grandfather learned his first Torah lessons from this very book, taught to him by his father. It has been in my family for over two hundred years."

"I thank you for sharing it with us," Pierre said quietly, speaking for them both.

Joseph Levy opened the book from what appeared to be the back cover, then Jake realized the writing was in the Hebrew script and thus printed from right to left. Joseph Levy showed them an opening page decorated to appear as a great medieval door. The sides were colonnaded and dressed with flowering vines, the base carved from stone, the roof crowned with light. The door was open, to reveal rows of Hebrew words. The bottom corner of the page was darkened and worn.

The old man turned the book back toward him, ran his forefinger across the top lines, and murmured the singsong cadence of something long memorized. He looked up and intoned, "*Barukh atah adonoy, lamdeni chukekha,*" and then in English, "Blessed be thou, O Lord; teach me thy statutes." He looked from one to the other and asked, "Can you tell me the source of these words?"

"The hundred and nineteenth Psalm," Jake said quietly.

Both men stared at him for a moment. Then Joseph

Levy gave a fraction of a nod. He placed his thumb upon the page's well-worn groove, and in a delicate practiced motion pushed the page up and over. The next page was entirely different, written in letters so small that from where Jake sat they appeared to be an almost solid block. Along the left-hand edge was a second, smaller column, almost like an afterthought. Joseph Levy reached to the tray and came up with something Jake had missed, a silver rod perhaps half again as long as his hand, so old and used that the scrollwork on the handle had been worn smooth. "One of you shall perhaps read for us the opening passage of the Book of Genesis. You may read from your Christian Bible."

Jake nodded to Pierre's silent enquiry. The Frenchman picked up his Bible and read, "In the beginning God created the heaven and the earth. And the earth was without form, and—"

"Stop, stop, the first passage only, I said." The old man's crossness had a different quality now, that of habit passed down over generations, a means of teaching with verve, with character. "It is just like the young of this day, wanting to take in all the Torah in one gulp. Hurry, hurry, hurry, a headlong rush to nowhere." He examined Pierre with frosty contempt. "Well, my young man in a hurry, those first ten words alone contain enough thought and mystery to occupy you for an entire lifetime."

Jake leaned back, thoroughly satisfied. This was going to be good. He just knew it.

"Listen and I will tell you. There was once a great king. His name was Talmi, you goyim knew him as Ptolemy. He inherited the crown of Egypt from Alexander the Great. In the year 3500, or 260 B.C. according to your count, Ptolemy discovered that none of the books in his vast library were able to satisfy his hunger for truth. He sent word to Jerusalem, requesting that people come to translate the Torah into Greek so that he could read it for himself. Seventy-two sages, six from each of the twelve tribes, made the journey. They carried with them the Books of Moses, written upon scrolls in gold ink. Real gold. The king thought this was done to honor him, but in truth it was because the sacred text was normally written and studied in black ink, and in this way they were handing over to a non-believer that which did not have the sanctity of the true Torah.

"The king received the wise men with all honors and great gifts. He set an entire island at their disposal and asked that they set about immediately translating the five Books of Moses into Greek. And here is where the hand of God showed itself. The king had made arrangements so that once upon the island, the wise men would not be able to converse either with each other or with the outside world. Ptolemy, you see, wanted *each* sage to translate the *entire* Torah."

It was only when the thumb lowered to the page corner and lifted and turned that Jake realized he was hearing a teaching from the inscribed text. Not once had the old man even glanced at the page before him, so well did he know the story.

"In this way, the king felt he would be able to tell the difference between what was human and what was divine within the sages' scrolls. The human would vary from person to person, and the divine would remain the same. And here is the first way we know that the great Lord intended this as a miraculous sign. Although the sages had no contact with each other, all seventy-two of them completed their work upon the same day. What is more, all five Books—the Books you call Genesis, Exodus, Leviticus, Numbers, and Deuteronomy—all were translated in just seventy days. And that is where the name for this translation comes, the Septuagint, the Seventy."

"We use that term as well," Jake offered.

"Of course you do. All the world, Christian and Jew alike, refer to this great work, yet who takes time to remember the miracle of its making? And the miracle does not end there. Oh no. It continues with what was written in those seventy-two translations.

"How do we know the Lord's hand was at work? Look at the words of the passage again. 'In the beginning God created the heavens.' But this is not how the Hebrew is written. Oh no. The original says, *Bereshith bara elohim,* which means literally, 'In the beginning created God.' But these sages, all working separately, decided that this would be misleading to someone who was not aware of the Hebrew tongue. They might think that someone or something called beginning had created the divine.

"And yet why did the Torah not simply say 'God created in the beginning'? Why was this so? Listen, and I will explain. It is because God is not like an earthly king, who wishes to be first and ahead of all others. No, God is in the middle of things. He is here with us, wherever we are, and the placing of His name was intended to show this."

The old man looked from one to the other, then said in quiet triumph, "And so it was that when the sages were brought back to the court of King Ptolemy, not only did they present him with *all* the books completed by *all* the sages upon the same day, but *every word of every translation was identical.* Not a difference was to be found, down to the smallest item. Thus did Ptolemy and all his court come to accept that the *entire* Torah was truly divine."

Again the unseen page shift, a pause for a sip from his glass, time enough for Pierre to cast an astonished glance in Jake's direction. Jake nodded his agreement. This was incredible.

"One more point, and then we in our modern hurry shall move on. Notice the word *beginning*. Now turn to the Book of Jeremiah, the second chapter, the third verse. Read this, one of you."

Jake found his place and read, "Israel was holiness unto the Lord, and the firstfruits of his increase."

"That is enough. Observe the word *firstfruits*. This in Hebrew is another word for beginnings. And so we see that Israel, the chosen people, were alluded to in the very first words of the Book of Genesis. The gracious Lord set them there at the onset of His divine teachings, reminding us for whom the words were spoken."

Another sip, then the dark eyes glanced from one man to the other and Joseph Levy asked, "Shall we continue?"

The knock, when it came, was so unexpected that all three men jumped. The door opened, and a worried Daniel Levy called from down the hall. "Papa? Miriam noticed your light was still on. Are you all right?"

"Of course I'm all right. Why shouldn't I be?"

Daniel Levy stepped into the room wearing a dark overcoat buttoned up over what appeared to be pajamas and slippers. "It's almost two o'clock in the morning. What are you doing?"

"Two o'clock? It can't be. We have not even finished the first chapter."

"First chapter of what?" He walked over, looked down at the book, and his eyes widened. "*Bereshith*? You are teaching them *Bereshith*?"

"Genesis," Joseph Levy corrected, rising slowly to his feet, testing each joint in turn. "They do not speak Hebrew, remember."

Jake tried to follow him up and realized only then that his back had locked into place. Pierre rose at an equally gradual pace. Jake said, "I guess we better be going."

"Yes you should," the son agreed, still scolding the father. "Miriam and I worry over you constantly, but when our backs are turned, look at what you do."

"There is nothing wrong with the teaching of Torah. A man does not grow ill studying the holy word."

"No," Daniel countered, supporting the old man with one hand on his arm. "A man becomes ill by staying up all hours of the night and not taking care of himself."

"This has been a great honor, Monsieur Levy," Pierre said gravely.

"I'd sure like to do this again," Jake said, then added for Daniel, "and I promise to watch the time."

Joseph brushed off his son's hands, turned to the pair, inspected the two faces. "Look at them, would you? Where have I seen that expression before?"

"Papa, it's late, and we must all—"

"I remember another face that shone after six and seven hours of study," the old man persisted. "A young boy who ate the words, who could not learn fast enough, who cried when it was time to halt."

Daniel's hand dropped back to his side. His beard moved up and down, but no word came.

"I remember," the old man continued, "a boy who would never leave me alone, who met me at the end of my most tiring day with pleas to open the sacred book, to teach him more of the stories and the mysteries of the words." Joseph pointed with one ancient, crooked finger at Jake. "Why do I remember? Because here before me are faces shining with that same hungry light. Minds and hearts so open to the words that the eyes illuminate the room."

Daniel glanced uncertainly toward Jake, his mouth opened slightly, the dark eyes questioning and vulnerable.

"Perhaps you should join us, my son," Joseph Levy said quietly. "Perhaps it would do you good to come and see these two eat the words as you once did, to join with us in the miracle of Scripture."

"With our wives," Jake said quietly, "if that would be all right."

"Of course with your wives," Joseph Levy agreed, yet kept his eyes upon his son. "For what is a family without the Holy Scripture to bond them?"

"It is late, Papa," Daniel Levy said weakly.

Jake and Pierre shook hands with the pair, then let themselves out. Silently they walked down the stairs, passed through the outer portal, and stepped out into the night. Only when they were back upon the lane, beneath the stars of another Istanbul night, did Pierre sigh and glance down at his feet. "How is it, my friend," he said to Jake, "that I can walk upon this tired and wounded earth while my mind and heart soar through the heavens above?"

Chapter Ten

J ake awoke to the smell of coffee and the sound of rustling papers.

He rolled over, sat up, and watched as Sally poured a cup and walked to the bedside. "You were so late coming in last night, I decided to let you sleep."

He nodded thanks, took a long sip, sighed at the pleasure of that first swallow. "I was at Daniel's. Pierre went with me."

"I saw your note." Her gaze was calm, resolute. "Jake, we have to talk."

The set of her chin and the sound of her voice called his fuzzy mind to attention. "Can I finish this first cup?"

"Just sit and listen." She took a breath, went on, "I know you said what you did because you love me and because you were worried. But you have to understand, I am who I am, just like you. I want you to live the life of adventure that you crave, but I have to be a part of it. Not waiting at home for you to return when it's over. I want to be there taking part *with* you."

Jake finished his cup and watched as she took it from him, walked back and refilled it, then returned to sit and hand it over and say, "This is the only way it is going to work."

"I know," he said quietly. "I knew it before I opened my mouth two nights ago."

"Let me finish. I have lived through too much and been on my own too long to ever be happy just sitting around, waiting for my man to come home."

"I wouldn't ever want you to be that way," he said, loving her.

She gave the mattress between them a muffled slap. "How am I supposed to argue with you if you keep agreeing with everything I say?"

"I don't want to argue with you," Jake replied. "Not ever again."

The resolute squaring of her chin softened a little, despite her best effort to keep it set. "You need me, Jake."

"More than anything," he agreed.

"I can be a big help to you."

"I could not get through a single day without you," he agreed.

The chin quivered, but this time with suppressed laughter. "And you love me. A lot."

"More than life itself," he agreed happily.

"So there won't be any more of this nonsense over where I go and what I do?"

"All the time," Jake countered. "I can't love you like I do and stop worrying. I just have to squelch my desire to give orders."

She flowed into him then, her arms welcoming, her gaze loving, her lips warm and tender. She kissed him, leaned back far enough to stroke his face, smile, and whisper, "Apology accepted," before embracing him again.

•   •   •

Sally watched him dress from her place on the bed, a habit of old which had somehow been misplaced during the clamor of their new assignment. Jake raised his collar, slid the tie into place, repeated the thought: *Their* new assignment. He turned toward her and reveled in the half-smile which played over her lips. Such an incredible lady.

He pointed down at the scroll of maps strewn over their table. "What's all this?"

"Oh, something I heard yesterday." She related her trip with Phyllis and the old couple's tale. "I had a lot of trouble even finding the place."

"What's it called?"

"Kumdare." She slid from the bed and walked over, her robe billowing about her. Jake straightened enough to watch as she leaned down, her reddish-gold hair spilling upon the page. She set a finger down, said, "Here it is."

He squinted to see an alien name perched upon a narrow spit of land. "Doesn't sound familiar."

"They said it was a tiny village, just one road in and out."

Jake knotted his tie, leaned over and tried to concentrate, but found it difficult with the closeness of her. He gave up, turned, and kissed her neck.

"Pay attention," she ordered, but hugged his arm to keep him close.

"Doesn't ring any bells."

"I know. But they were so insistent that the Americans were paying for this construction project."

"Kumdare," he repeated, committing the name to memory. He studied the map again. The tiny village rested upon an empty elbow of land. The place appeared utterly isolated, situated at the other end of the Bosphorus, at the point where the strait opened into the Black Sea. "It's miles from anywhere."

"I know." She straightened and wrapped her arms around him. "There's not much time left, is there?"

"Less than two days," he said as lightly as he could manage, not wanting the moment to end just yet. "According to what Fernwhistle said in the meeting, the dispatch should arrive sometime tomorrow."

"I'm supposed to meet with Phyllis this morning. She's trying to set something up, I don't know what."

"So it's Phyllis now, is it."

Sally nodded, still distracted. "Jasmyn's already left for someplace called the Sophia Mosque, I think I've got that right. She's meeting the woman who took us through the palace." She looked up at him. "If we find out anything, should we come by the consulate?"

Jake sighed and gave in as the pressures rose to surround him. "You can try. I don't know where I'll be." He sketched out what he had learned yesterday, including his meetings at the construction site and opposition headquarters.

Sally listened with increasing seriousness. "You have to watch out as well, Jake."

"I know."

"These people aren't going to just let you walk off with their fat little contracts."

"I'll be careful, Sally."

"Especially if they're pocketing part of the proceeds." She started to wring her hands, looked down and saw what she was doing, searched for the pockets to her robe. "Promise me you won't do anything rash."

"I've already arranged for backup," he said, and explained about the Marine guards.

"Well, they won't do any good unless you take them along." She reached for him again, a grip intensified with fear and love. "Go," she whispered, "and come back safe."

Jake entered his office and said to Daniel in greeting, "Ever heard of a place called Kumdare?"

Daniel froze, one hand deep inside the last of the unsorted boxes. "How did you know?"

The stance and the tone were all the warning Jake needed. Quietly he shut the outer door, walked over, spoke more quietly, "Know what?"

"One bill I have found, just one. And just this morning." Daniel eased himself upright. "But already you have heard of it."

"A rumor," Jake said, and told him what Sally had learned.

Long wax-colored fingers rose to stroke his beard. "You think maybe this is the project our opponents wish to keep hidden?"

"I don't know. Maybe. You say there's a bill?"

"Just one. But the largest so far. A requisition, really, simply confirming that payment was required for work done up to . . ." Daniel searched through the clutter on his desk, came up with a single hand-written invoice, finished, ". . . the beginning of last week. For a cultural center, or so it says here."

"Have you ever heard of this place?"

"Never." Daniel shook his head, his eyes not leaving Jake's face. "All my life I have lived and worked in Istanbul, and this village is unknown to me."

"How are the roads outside Istanbul?"

"Very bad," Daniel replied without hesitation. "And to the smaller villages, even worse."

"Strange place to set up a center for anything," Jake mused, then decided, "Go downstairs and see if you can set up a priority call to London. It's time I had another chat with Harry Grisholm."

"Once, this great city was called Byzantium, a small Greek fishing village on a naturally protected outcrop of land. Then it became Constantinople, home to the last Roman emperors and center of the civilized world. Later came the Islamic invasion and the Ottoman Empire. Now it is a city clinging to the edge of Western civilization, an uneasy mix of cultures and histories."

Jasmyn nodded and kept her face politely alert as they walked at a measured pace through the rubble-strewn parkland. Jana played the cheerful tour guide, one of many leading groups or individuals along the crowded lanes. "At its height, the palace begun by Constantine had five hundred public halls and thirty chapels. All that is left now is this ragged garden, these crumbling walls and pillars, and these fading mosaics set in what is now a field of rubble."

They crossed the grand square and walked toward the Sophia Mosque, joining a throng of chattering pilgrims. As they climbed the stairs, Jasmyn followed Jana's example and tied a kerchief about her head. Inside, the great dome seemed almost translucent, with decorations as delicate as a painting upon porcelain. The grand expanse of floor was cushioned by multiple layers of carpets. The light was filtered and gentle and as still as the dust which drifted in the air.

"The Church of Aga Sophia was originally built fifteen hundred years ago by the Emperor Justinian." Jana examined the younger woman and asked, "You are Christian, yes?"

"I am."

"Does it trouble you to see that such ancient churches are now mosques?"

"A little." Jasmyn reined in her impatience and looked to where a giant mosaic of Mary and the Christ child decorated one wall of the upper balcony. The walls around it were scarred by what appeared from that distance to be sword thrusts, as though ancient warriors had scraped off all but that one lonely mosaic. To either side, towering pillars supported great black shields twice the height of a man, upon which were emblazoned Arabic script in fiery gold. Directly overhead, the great dome seemed to hover in space. "At least the structure is still here."

"Indeed so. This mighty building has survived lootings, wars, and earthquakes. In fact, it is built upon the foundations of a church erected two hundred years earlier by Constantine himself. That church was destroyed by a fire." Jana pointed about at other mosaics, half-figures whose faces had been left while their bodies were destroyed, prophets reaching out across the centuries, and scarred images of the risen Christ. "There were great arguments about these, as Islam forbids the making of images. But any which were somewhat hidden, like those in the upper balconies, and all that depicted prophets shared by both Islam and Christianity were permitted to remain."

Jana led Jasmyn toward the front, saying, "When the church was converted to a mosque, fragments of the Byzantine furnishings were kept and used." She pointed to the pulpit, the entrance adorned with a velvet drape embossed with Arabic script. "That pulpit, for example, is twelve hundred years old. And these carpets cover a vast array of Byzantine mosaics."

Jasmyn took a deep breath of air laden with dusty age and asked quietly, "Are we being followed?"

"I cannot say for certain," Jana said, and smiled brightly as she pointed out one of the great black shields. "But I fear so."

Jasmyn nodded and tried to hold her attention where the tour guide directed. "Why are we here?"

"Are you aware of a village called Kumdare?"

Jasmyn started at the word, recalling her conversation with Sally the night before. "Why do you ask?"

Jana threw her a shrewd glance before returning her attention to the gold-encrusted dome. "It is good to be cautious with strangers such as myself. Kumdare is the name of a village on the Asiatic coast. The Americans are supposed to be building there. For some reason, the Russians have taken great interest in this project." She dropped her arm, turned, and smiled with false animation. "Whatever it is that you seek, it appears that you may find the answer there. Only take care. The Russians will do anything to protect their secrets."

"Jake!" Harry Grisholm's cheery tone rose above the telephone's crackling static. "How nice to hear from you. How are you, my boy?"

"Well as can be expected," Jake shouted back. "When are you arriving?"

"I still cannot say for certain, but I am pushing hard as possible for sometime early next week."

"No good." Jake gave a succinct version of the pressures he faced, then stopped and listened to the static. "Harry?"

"I'm still here, my boy." For once the almost constant cheeriness had failed him. "It sounds as though they have us both over the diplomatic barrel."

"Sure looks that way to me," Jake agreed. "Have you ever heard of some project we're supposed to be financing at Kumdare?"

A second silence ensued, cut off by Harry saying, "Now that you mention it, something about a cultural center. Do I recall correctly?"

"That's what I have here," Jake called back. "But why—"

"Absolutely unimportant," Harry cut him off. "What is *extremely vital* is that you keep a *watchful eye*. Are you reading me, Jake?"

"I'm not sure," he said, scrambling to locate a pen and paper. "You're saying this center at Kumdare—"

"Is totally insignificant." Even the crackling line could not disguise the sudden tension in Harry's voice. "You recall our previous conversation, my boy?"

"About listening in."

"Precisely. I *command* you to *watch* carefully and use your *post* to *observe*. Then, whatever happens, you can return from this with useful lessons. Are you following me?"

"Trying hard," he said, writing out those words to which Harry had given special emphasis.

"Very good. There is little time left, Jake. I am counting on you to hold to what is of the *utmost importance*."

"You can count on me," Jake said, inserting a confidence he did not feel.

"I have no choice, so long as my hands remain tied here. Take care, my gallant friend, and remember me to your charming wife."

Jake looked down at the words he had scribbled and shouted, "Daniel!"

The bearded face appeared in the doorway, inspected him, declared, "You have learned something."

"Maybe." Jake reread the words on his paper. "If I understood him correctly, it's not going to be a cultural center at all. It's a command post. For observation."

Daniel stared at him. "Observation of what?"

"That's what I intend to find out." Jake sprang for the door. "I've got to run for that meeting with Turgay. You try and contact Pierre Servais at the French embassy. Go over there in person, don't trust the phones. Tell him we leave in two hours." Jake was halfway through the outer office before turning back around and saying to the utterly baffled young man, "And if you can get either Adams or Bailey of the Marine detachment alone, tell them the exact same thing."

Chapter Eleven

Sally rushed down one cobblestone lane after another. With each step she grew more certain that she had gone astray from Phyllis Hollamby's directions. Domes and minarets poked through Istanbul's perpetual cover of dust and noise. The city wore a scruffy look, as though the builders were in such a hurry to move on that nothing was ever quite finished and no one had time to clean up afterward. But the vibrancy was stronger than anywhere Sally had ever been, an electric quality that caught her early in the morning and held her tight in its excited grip all day.

Faces in the crowd were dark and Oriental and extremely friendly. Sally finally stopped an old man and asked for directions. He rewarded her with a great beam of welcome and a stream of Turkish. He then proceeded to halt a well-heeled woman carrying a shopping bag. She too gave a smile in Sally's direction. That proved to be not enough, so she walked over and gave Sally's hand an energetic pumping, then offered another stream of unintelligible words, followed by a great hoot of laughter shared with the old man. They then stopped a third person, and then a fourth, until within five minutes Sally was surrounded by a crowd

of some fifteen people, all smiling and kindly chattering away to her and pointing in fifteen different directions.

Eventually one elderly woman took her hand, and
with a gap-toothed smile gently led her down the
street in the same direction from which she had come.

"Spice market," Sally insisted.

The woman responded with a great smile and more
Turkish, tugging her cheerfully along the crowded
lane.

Five minutes later Sally was rewarded with a
cheery, "Ah, there you are, my dear. How utterly splendid." Phyllis smiled at the old woman still holding to
Sally's hand. "Busy making friends, are we?"

"I got lost, and she adopted me."

Phyllis exchanged a stream of conversation with
the delighted old woman, who would only go after
having given Sally's hand yet another shake, then kiss-
ing her on the cheek. Phyllis waved as she walked off,
and said to Sally, "This ability of yours to make friends
will serve you well, my dear. Is the delightful Jasmyn
still with Jana?"

"I guess so. She is supposed to meet us here when
she is done."

"Splendid." Phyllis turned toward the entrance of
what appeared to be a stubby brick warehouse with
three central domes. "Well, then, perhaps we should
begin."

The extended roofline cut a dark swathe through
the gathering heat. Phyllis led her into the welcoming
shade and told her, "When Egypt fell to the Ottomans,
suddenly a flood of exotic roots, seeds, fruits, and
spices appeared along the docks of Istanbul. That gave

rise to the Egyptian Market, or Spice Market as it is also known today."

Sally allowed herself to be led inside, and discovered that the warehouse was neither square nor short, as the exterior suggested. Instead, the grand colonnaded hall extended in three vast lanes, the vaulted ceiling rising forty feet above her head. Crowded around the ancient columns were shops selling everything from oranges to ground cumin. The air was heavy with the fragrance of cinnamon, coriander, bay leaf, and lavender.

"The building was originally made of wood," Phyllis continued merrily. "But gunpowder was sold here as a cure for hemorrhoids, and too many of the stalls kept blowing holes in the old roof. So three hundred years ago the sultan had it rebuilt in stone. They did a lovely job, don't you agree?"

"You make it sound like it all happened yesterday," Sally replied.

"If you wish to make Istanbul a part of yourself, you must treat time as the city does. Days and weeks and months and years and even centuries will gradually begin to melt together before your very eyes."

Sally examined the older woman. "Why are you helping us out so much?"

"Because I have absolutely nothing else to fill my days."

"I find that hard to believe."

"It is true nonetheless." Phyllis raised her free hand to the side of her face. In that simple motion, all her years lay exposed. The hand was age-spotted, the fingers shook gently, and they missed the first time they wiped at the damp that gathered at the corner of her mouth. "My George perished seven years ago. I started to return to England, but my goodness, since I have lived all my adult life out here, what on earth was I to return to?"

"You don't have any children?"

"One daughter. She lives in Portsmouth and complains of how her dear mama refuses to simply lie down and give up the ghost, as she feels all elderly old windbags should do upon demand."

"You are not that elderly," Sally replied, liking her tremendously. "And most certainly not a windbag."

"Thank you, my dear. But I do confess, were it not for my inner source of strength and the occasional opportunity to make a difference in this way, life and this burden of years would simply be too much for me to bear. I have always been active, you see. It is this feeling that I still have something worthy to contribute that keeps me going."

Sally waved as Jasmyn came into view and said to Phyllis, "You have certainly contributed to making things better for us since we came. We can't thank you enough."

"I have done it as much for myself as for you," Phyllis replied, smiling a welcome to Jasmyn. "By giving, I am rewarded beyond measure. Freely I have received, freely will I give on to others."

Sally stared at the older woman. "You are a believer?"

"I try my best to follow the Lord's call." She turned to Jasmyn, asked, "How are you, my dear?"

"Troubled," she replied, her beautiful face clouded.

"Yes, that I can most certainly see. Alas, that is the problem of dealing with anything tainted by the Russians these days. They do so love to stir the waters with trouble and intrigue."

"But I did not mention the Russians."

"You did not need to." Phyllis Hollamby turned both women around by starting down the central hall herself. "Unfortunately, their interest in Turkey has become almost suffocating. Identify any distressing crisis, and you will most likely find the Soviets at work."

"And this Jana," Jasmyn demanded. "You are sure we can trust her?"

"Ah, she had information for you, did she? Excellent. Yes, Jana is a remarkable young woman. Her father worked as office assistant to my husband, and we have helped with the cost of her education. She is doing further work in political science and will someday be a force to be reckoned with, mark my words. She is fiercely patriotic and sees the Soviets as the greatest single threat to her country's future. Yes indeed, you may certainly trust her and any information she manages to gather on your behalf."

As they walked by one brilliant display after another, Jasmyn outlined what she had heard from the young woman. Phyllis heard her out, then pointed them toward a stall with the words, "Let us hear what this friend has to say, shall we?"

Sally followed her over, asked doubtfully, "And then?"

"And then, my dear, we shall find it time to make a decision." Phyllis beamed as the wizened stallholder doffed his cap and bowed at their approach. He stood among wicker baskets piled high with ground spices, their odors a pungent perfume. There were clove and coriander, cumin and curry, pepper and basil and bay, all the colors and smells of the Orient. The man was as timeless as the market, aged somewhere between forty and eighty, his grin almost toothless and his eyes almost lost in leathery folds. Phyllis pointed toward several piles, and the man used a small scoop to fill one bag after another, weighing each on an ancient scale using tiny copper weights, arguing politely with her over prices. He filled the intervals with murmured snatches of conversation, a flurry of words that gradually tightened both their faces, until Phyllis finally pressed money into his hand and turned from his final bow with a taut smile.

Sally waited until they had moved away before demanding quietly, "What is the matter?"

"Smile, my dear, and look interested in the displays," Phyllis said, her voice overly bright. "He says there are eyes upon us."

"Jana said the same thing," Jasmyn said.

"Don't look so worried, dear. We are just a trio of foreigners enjoying a day of sightseeing and shopping." Phyllis nodded approval as Jasmyn released a blithe little laugh. "Excellent. In anticipation of this, and from what we learned yesterday, I took my car across on the first ferry this morning. I also took the liberty of packing a lunch for us."

She smiled and pointed toward a display that none of them saw. "This way I hope we shall be off and away while our footsore followers are still searching for a vehicle."

"You are truly amazing," Sally said quietly.

"Thank you, my dear. Now, you must hurry back to the hotel and leave a note for your husbands. Say simply that we have gone for a drive down the coast."

Sally resisted the urge to search the surrounding crowds. "Where are we going?"

"It is time," Phyllis replied, "for us to see what lies within this village called Kumdare."

•   •   •

The Flower Market was a vast domed building that resembled the inside of a palace, all ornate porticoes and grand mirrors and chandeliers and windows taller than Jake. The building stood upon a steep-sided hill looking down over the glistening waters of the Golden Horn. Beyond its waters rose the thrilling prospect of the old city and all its mysteries.

A chamber opening to one side had been turned into an eating hall. There, fragrances of well-spiced food mingled with those of the flowers to create an intoxicating bouquet.

Jake walked over to where Turgay Ecevit was seated and shook the proffered hand. "Sorry I'm late."

"Do not bother to apologize, Mr. Burnes. Diplomats are always expected to be delayed. It adds importance to their posts, being able to claim some grave diplomatic crisis."

Jake seated himself and replied, "In this case, it's the truth."

"No doubt, no doubt." He showed jolly disbelief. "I have taken the liberty of ordering a small meal for us. I hope that is acceptable."

"Great. I missed breakfast and I'm starved." The waiter appeared, clad in a ballooning white shirt and a multicolored vest. He set down plate after miniature plate until their table was crowded with a dozen small dishes.

"Mezze," Turgay explained. "It means a thousand dishes."

There were two different kinds of lamb, on skewers and grilled with peppers and pine nuts. There was salad of diced fennel and basil, beans both cold and hot and all heavily spiced, yogurt mixed with a variety of ingredients, and triangular pastries filled with cheese or spinach or meat. Fish and shrimp and shellfish made up the remaining portions, all swimming in spiced garlic oil. Jake surveyed the feast. "A small meal?"

"Wait, there is more," Turgay said, and suddenly the air grew pungent with woodsmoke and roasting lamb. A chef and his assistant rolled over a great wooden trolley with a revolving vertical spit. The lamb was layered thick as a man's reach, and the charcoal banked in an upright grill. The spit was turned slowly, the outer blackened layer stripped off with a knife longer than Jake's arm, then caught in a frying pan with a wedge cut out so that it fit up snug to the spit. Jake watched as the meat was set upon an oval platter and covered in a layer of spicy tomato sauce, then with another layer of meat, a layer of yogurt, and a final layer of meat, and the entire dish topped with diced onions and fragrant herbs. The mustachioed chef set down the plate with a flourish, then added two platter-sized loaves of fresh unleavened bread.

"Bursa kebab," Turgay announced proudly. "A favorite of mine."

Jake allowed his plate to be heaped high, tasted, pronounced it all delicious.

While they ate, a troupe of musicians wandered through the hall. To Jake's mind, Turkish music was the most thoroughly Oriental part of the culture. A half-dozen drums and tambourines kept up a complex beat while the remaining instruments joined in constant discord and the singing rose strident above it all. The overall effect was as exotic and flavorful as the food.

Over cups of treacly thick coffee, Turgay produced

a sheaf of papers from his coat pocket. "I have pre-pared the list as you ordered."

"I do not," Jake responded, "make it a habit to order around a foreign government—or even members of the opposition party."

"You hold the purse strings," Turgay reminded him. "That adds great power to any request." He un-folded the sheets. "There are five companies which we could identify in the time you gave us."

Jake peered over the list. "All are large enough to handle construction projects of this size?"

"All have already done so," Turgay answered. "When will you have the bidding documents ready?"

"Maybe never," Jake said, and decided the least he could do was explain the time pressure he faced. As he described the recent developments, he refolded the documents and tried to settle them into his jacket pocket. "Having a list of companies that could have been sent tenders will make good ammunition, but I've still got to find something big enough to blow a breach in their defenses. And fast."

Turgay nodded his understanding, pointed at what Jake held, asked, "What is that?"

Jake looked down and realized he had pulled out his New Testament to make room for the papers. "I like to carry a Bible with me."

"Ah, a Christian." Turgay smiled approval. "I have often wanted to argue the points of this religion."

It hit him then, a sudden sense of the answer pre-pared and waiting. "I will not argue with anyone," Jake replied quietly yet firmly. "Not over this."

Turgay shrugged his disregard. "Discuss, then."

"Not that, either." Jake pressed the documents flat-ter, fitted his New Testament back out of sight.

The outright rejection confused the handsome young man. "This is a most curious matter, Mr. Burnes. If it is so important that you carry this book with you always, why will you not discuss religion with me?"

"Because it is not just a religion to me," Jake replied. "It is my *faith*. It is the bedrock of my life. Faith is not something that can be shared through intellectual debate. You can't hold it out at arm's length and analyze it and come away understanding anything."

"Most remarkable," Turgay murmured.

"If you want to hear the message of salvation, I would be happy to share my experience. If you wish to speak of the ache of an empty heart, I would be privileged to listen and share with you what faith has done in my own life. If you would like to pray with me, I would be honored to bow my head with yours."

Turgay drummed his fingers on the table, clearly ill at ease with the direction the discussion had taken. "Perhaps we should return to the matter at hand."

"Fine with me." Jake settled back, content. He had made the offer, planted the seed. It was up to the Lord now to perform His miracle.

Chapter Twelve

"Are you a believer as well, my dear?" Phyllis directed the question into her rearview mirror without slowing a fraction.

"I have witnessed far too many miracles," Jasmyn replied faintly, her face blanched, her eyes pinned to the vista sweeping by outside her window, "not to believe in God."

"So very glad to hear it," Phyllis said gaily. "So very glad."

The road, such as it was, wound its way higher and higher up a cliffside flanking the Bosphorus. Sally tried as hard as she could not to look to their left. Blue sky swooped down a terrifying distance to sparkling blue waters below. Occasionally the road leveled and curved away from the sea, entering one hard-scrabble village after another. Phyllis did not slow a fraction from her headlong rush, but scattered chickens and goats and donkey carts and villagers with true British aplomb.

"Faith is a marvelous addition to one's life," Phyllis said, utterly blind to the effect her driving was having on her two passengers. "I simply cannot imagine what I would have done after George's untimely demise had

I not had my faith to shelter me."

The car was a truly enormous Citroen, the long snout a perfect wedge for Phyllis's form of driving, which consisted primarily of setting the course and allowing everyone else to simply get out of her way. In place of turn signals, two great flaps extended alongside the doors. When Phyllis wished to turn, she pushed one of two levers on her sculpted chrome dash, and the metal flag flapped out and down with a bong from the signal bell. The problem was, Phyllis neglected to bother with the flags until she was already spinning her wheel. And she used her rearview mirror only for talking with the passenger in the backseat. Their journey was therefore punctuated by horns and screeching brakes and shouts fading into the distance. Sally had long since given up turning around to survey the chaos. All she could see in their wake was a great, billowing dust cloud.

Phyllis came within inches of jamming a donkey cart over the cliff, spun the wheel, and blithely slipped into the path of an oncoming truck, then just as swiftly slid back in front of the cart. As the braying donkey, shouting driver, and honking truck faded into the distance, Phyllis declared proudly, "Almost there, ladies. You can see the village on that next crest up ahead."

"Praise be to the Lord above," Jasmyn said faintly from the backseat.

"Now, then." Spurred by the sight of their destination, Phyllis pressed down upon the accelerator, and the great motor beneath the long black hood roared in delight. Sally slid another notch down in the overpadded seat as Phyllis continued briskly, "You must recall that we are here as tourists, simply visiting a quaint little fishing village."

Sally closed her eyes as the far wheels skidded around a curve, sending a spray of rocks cascading down to distant waters. "You're sure this speed is necessary?"

"Why of course, my dear," Phyllis replied, misunderstanding her totally. "You yourself have said that the letter dismissing your husband will arrive sometime tomorrow."

"She meant," Jasmyn tried feebly, "must we drive so fast?"

"Always best to outrun trouble, I say." Phyllis spun the wheel with the ease of one raised on hairpin turns. "You will both be happy to know I have never had an accident."

"And never will have but one," Sally replied, but her words were lost in yet another truck's blaring horn.

"We must follow up any lead we have," Phyllis said, returning to the matter at hand. "The spice trader's story was the third bit of evidence pointing toward Kumdare. Where there's smoke there's fire, I say, especially when the Russians are fanning the flames."

The spice trader bought from several local markets in the region around Kumdare, and twice he had heard of foreigners buying provisions. Pale-skin foreigners who spoke smatterings of Turkish with a distinctly Russian accent, and who never returned to the same market twice. Their presence was remarkable enough to cause talk.

Phyllis rounded the final bend, swooped down and into the unsuspecting village, halted in a paved courtyard, and cut the engine. Then she turned and beamed at her two passengers. "Now, that wasn't so bad, was it?"

• • •

The cicadas hummed a constant refrain to the heat and the sun. Their buzz seemed to make the air even hotter. The road they walked was little more than a narrow gravel path between crumbling stone walls, with the sun and twin minarets for direction markers.

"This village was a way station for travelers two thousand years ago," Phyllis told them as they walked. "Traders would harness their pack animals in a circle around their goods, then sleep outside them in double rows for security."

Old men sat and stared at their passage, fingering amber worry beads. Children scampered and giggled and pointed at the oddity of foreign women in their midst. The village girls were quick and as pretty as tiny porcelain dolls, dressed in brightly colored dresses and miniature headkerchiefs.

They entered the central square, where a local market attracted a crowd of chattering, haggling locals. Squinting against the fierce sun, Sally ignored the glances tossed their way and inspected her surroundings. The village had been constructed to endure the heat in comfort. Verandas were broad and built around great sheltering trees, the multitude of branches offering far more protection than mere roofs. Outer walls more than three feet thick offered substantial barriers to the heat. Restaurants and teahouses were open affairs, tables spread out on the verandas, beckoning diners into their shadowy cool depths.

Sally turned to Jasmyn and observed, "You look a little queasy."

"So do you." She tried for a smile. "I do not look forward to the trip back."

"Me, neither," Sally agreed. "Now that we're here, I wonder what we're supposed to do."

"Whatever it is," Jasmyn said, "it is bound to attract attention. I feel eyes upon us everywhere."

"Yoo-hoo, ladies," Phyllis called and waved. "Over here, if you please."

Sally started to complain that her feet were already begging loudly for a rest and the sun was sweltering, but Phyllis beckoned impatiently. She sighed and gave Jasmyn a minute shrug. Together they walked over to where a man was poking a metal rod down the mouth of a broad wooden cylinder. Phyllis smiled at her approach and announced, "I have just what you need."

"What I need," Sally said, "is a nice, cool bath."

"And some shade," Jasmyn added.

"I believe you might like this even better." Phyllis turned to the man, who despite the heat wore a voluminous shirt, a vest sewn with bits of reflecting glass, and a tall fez. She said to them, "Step closer, if you will."

"What for?" But Sally did as she was told and instantly was consumed by a wave of coolness. She gaped, bringing a delighted laugh from both Phyllis and the throng of children who now surrounded them. The man grinned but did not stop with his energetic stirring. Sally leaned over the cylinder to gaze down the narrow opening and saw a white, doughy ball at the base. She felt the coolness even more strongly. Sally stepped aside so that Jasmyn could take a look and demanded, "What on earth?"

"You will see." Phyllis chattered to the man, who gave a mock half-bow, reached for a small metal plate, raised his long rod, and scraped off some of the dough. Instantly the surrounding children were clamoring for attention, their faces and voices a mixture of pleading and laughter.

Phyllis plucked a spoon from a glass on the ledge, then handed the serving to Sally. "Taste."

Gingerly she touched a tiny portion to her tongue and exclaimed, "Ice cream!"

The children squealed with delight and absolutely butchered the words in an attempt to imitate Sally's surprise. Phyllis handed Jasmyn a plate, accepted her own portion, and said, "This gentleman travels from village to village all summer long. You can hear the bells on his little truck a mile or so off. Nowadays this cylinder is packed with dry ice, but when my children were young he came in a cart with straw packed around great bales of ice. The day he visited our area was something they looked forward to all year long."

Sally took another tiny scoop and watched as Phyllis gave the man a handful of coins and began doling out ice cream to all the surrounding children. Their excitement was so great they could scarcely stand still long enough to accept the little metal platters. Phyllis calmed them with a gentle tone, her face suddenly unlined, her eyes as bright as the children's. When the last child had been fed and the last whimpering plea stilled, Sally asked, "You mentioned having children, but I thought you told me that you only have one daughter."

"That's right, dear." She smiled in reply to the chorus of delighted giggles. "My son was killed in the war. That was the George I referred to earlier, when I said faith had proven so important to me. My husband, God rest his soul, had endured two years of a lingering illness before he was taken, and the dear man was ready to go. George was another matter entirely." Her tone was bright, her voice matter of fact, but the pain formed two deep holes at the center of her gaze. "George was a pilot. We lost him in the Battle of Britain."

"I'm so very sorry," Jasmyn said for them both.

"Thank you. You are both such dears." She looked back down to the eager little faces, gained strength from their joy. The gaze tightened, focused. "George gave his life so that we might enjoy this wonderful gift of freedom. I feel it is my duty as his mother to continue where he left off. Which brings us to the matter of our journey today."

Phyllis leaned upon her cane and lowered her head close to the children. She asked them a question. A chorus of little voices piped up in reply. The ice cream vendor added his own basso agreement, nodding vigorously and pointing off in the same direction as the multitude of smaller hands. Phyllis half spoke, half sung another query, and instantly the children were on their feet, licking the metal platters shiny-clean, handing them and the spoons back to the vendor, all of them grasping now for a hand of Sally or Jasmyn or Phyllis.

Surrounded by eagerly chattering children, the women were led out of the square, down a side street, and beyond the tight cluster of central buildings. The farther they walked, the more dispersed grew the dwellings, with farm animals bleating over the children's animated chatter. Above and to the right, away from the water's glittering surface, rose a rocky hillside. The ridgeline bore an ancient stone city wall, the parapets rising like uneven teeth. The women were led through a tumbledown opening, the flanking pillars all that was left of what once had been a mighty city gate. Beyond that point, the way became little more than a cattle track. Sally forced her way through the eager children to take Phyllis's free hand and help her over the rougher patches.

By the time they made it over the second hill, all three women were breathing hard. The children gathered about them at the crest, pointed forward, and competed loudly for the privilege of telling the story.

Sally looked down the swooping distance to where the hill joined the cliffside and fell in rocky jaggedness to the sea. They were at the highest point within sight, and the view was awesome. The Bosphorus shimmered like a brilliant blue mirror more than a thousand feet below. In the distance, the narrow strait's opposite shore rose like pale, frozen waves.

Phyllis shushed the clamoring children, turned her attention back to the vista, said, "I believe we have found our answer, ladies."

Sally nodded agreement. The hilltop was marked by a series of small surveyor flags, and three piles of earth and stone marked the beginning of squared-off cellar pits, but otherwise nothing had been done. Yet the structure's intended purpose was alarmingly clear.

Jasmyn pointed toward the horizon. "Look, there!"

Sally squinted against the harsh sunlight, felt her chest fill with a sharply indrawn breath. Steaming toward both them and the Bosphorus's narrow entrance passage were seven enormous ships. Each silhouette sprouted over two dozen menacing gun barrels. And streaming out behind every central smokestack flew a flag.

"The hammer and sickle," Jasmyn breathed.

"Soviet battleships," Sally agreed.

"Come, ladies," Phyllis said, returning to brisk urgency. "We have news to convey."

Chapter Thirteen

W atch out!"
Pierre drove wide around the horse-
drawn hay wagon, sliding back into place before the
oncoming truck could do more than clip his front
fender. He sounded genuinely affronted as he said,
"You are feeling more nervous than usual, perhaps?"

"The idea," Jake replied, "is to arrive there in one
piece."

"First you tell me to hurry, and now you want me
to slow down?" Pierre shook his head. "Perhaps you
would be more comfortable in the backseat."

Jake jammed both feet down on an imaginary brake
pedal as Pierre swung the heavy consular vehicle
around a ninety-degree bend, spewing gravel off the
road and over the cliff and down the several hundred
feet to the sea far below. "Maybe we should have taken
the consulate's driver after all."

"I thought the idea was to go in secrecy," Pierre replied, not slowing even a little. "And to do so with all
possible haste."

"We won't be able to give them much help lying at
the bottom of the sea."

"Let us hope," Pierre replied, accelerating to an

even faster pace, "that they do not need our help at all."

Jake had returned to the consulate from his meeting with Turgay to find both Pierre and the two Marines ready and chomping at the bit. At Jake's insistence, they took two cars minus drivers. The Marines were ordered to follow a few cars back and see if anyone tried to follow. Any move toward them, and the Marines were ordered to take what Jake called extreme evasive tactics. At the words, grins sprouted from both soldiers.

It was not until they stopped by the hotel on their way out of town that panic set in. Jake came racing out of his room and almost collided with an equally frantic Pierre. Jake looked at the sheet of paper his friend was waving. "I don't believe this is happening."

"Kumdare," Pierre groaned. "By themselves."

"Did they leave a time of departure?"

"It does not matter," Pierre said, too impatient to wait for the clanking elevator, taking the stairs in three-step leaps. "They are ahead of us and without protection. That is all we need to know."

Pierre glanced over to where Jake kept a death's grip on both the side armrest and dash. "You are beginning to make me tense."

Jake shot an exasperated look at his friend. "I can't tell you how sorry I am to hear it."

"Blinders," Pierre said, taking a curve wide and fast, sweeping back just in time to avoid attaching them to an ancient bus which itself took the swerve like a boat on high seas. "I knew I had forgotten something."

Jake forced himself to turn away from the precipice, tried not to think how naked it looked without a guardrail—just an empty void dropping out and down to distant rocks and glittering sea. He watched through his side window as the Turkish afternoon blurred past. Dark mustachioed men and kerchiefed women driving donkey carts piled like miniature mountains. Villages anchored by needle-slim minarets. Mud-brick walls, dusty children, bleating animals, metal roofs. Then rows and rows of carefully cultivated crops, distinguished at their speed more by smell than sight. Vineyards, olive groves, herb gardens, vegetable patches, all tilled in the timeless manner by human labor and wooden implements.

"Car wrecks," Jake observed. "There's one at almost every curve."

Pierre jammed on the brakes, swerved, slowed long enough to trade compliments with a Turkish driver, then sped on. "I agree. These people know nothing of proper driving." He plowed through a flock of sheep, carefully avoided the shepherd's flaying staff, finished, "Which is another reason why one must drive quickly. Any slower and trouble would have time to catch up with us."

Jake sighed his way deeper into the seat, decided if he watched much more, he would not survive long enough to live through an accident. He crossed his arms, closed his eyes, and gave his fate grimly over to God.

Jake awoke with a start to the sound of screeching tires and blaring horns. To his vast relief, his eyes focused in time to tell him that all the noise belonged to other vehicles. He rubbed his face. "I fell asleep."

"For almost an hour," Pierre crowed triumphantly. "A grand testimony to my perfect driving."

"That's impossible," Jake said, trying to shake the remnants of sleep from his brain. "It can't have happened."

"While you rested in my watchful care, I have discovered the secret of driving in Turkey," Pierre declared.

Jake searched through his window, observed dismally, "We're not there yet?"

"It is quite simple," Pierre continued. "The most important rule is, there are no rules!"

"I suppose that makes sense," Jake said, "to a Frenchman."

"Exactly!" Pierre blithely ignored a truck that was trying to cut into the stream of traffic from a side road by jamming its snout far into the road. Pierre simply swerved into the face of an oncoming vehicle, then swept back and continued smugly, "Once you understand this, the rest is quite simple."

Jake raised himself up, suddenly more awake than he had ever been in his life. "Any sign of the Marines?"

"One car back," Pierre said, risking a glance in the rearview mirror. "I must say, that corporal certainly does know how to drive."

For once, Jake was not sorry when traffic suddenly snarled, leaving them crawling forward through an overheated cloud of diesel fumes. They entered yet another village, one removed from time, sheltered in groves of hazelnut and beech. To one side, men turned an ancient concrete mixer and piled bricks beside an unfinished house, all by hand. To the other, tobacco leaves hung on a clothesline to dry. Underneath scrabbled a flock of scrawny chickens.

Pierre smiled at nothing, asked, "Do you remember Vera Lynn?"

Jake turned away from the window. "What?"

" 'We'll meet again, don't know where, don't know when,' " Pierre sang in a truly atrocious voice. "Do you not remember that, my friend?"

"I can't believe I'm hearing a Frenchman ask me that."

"Vera Lynn," Pierre sighed. "She sang for the heart of every Frenchman as we fled the German invasion of Paris."

"I hate to spoil a good memory," Jake told him. "But Vera wasn't singing for the French."

"No?" Pierre mulled that one over for a moment, then shrugged. "Well, she should have been."

"I'll be sure to pass that along the next time I see her," Jake assured him.

"And Dooley Wilson. What was that wonderful song of his, 'As Time Goes By'?"

"No more singing," Jake begged. "And it was originally Satchmo's song."

Pierre gave him an astonished glance. "You do not care for my voice?"

"Let's just say it runs a close second to your driving," Jake said.

"And 'Moonlight Serenade,' ah, that was a lovely one."

"What's gotten you taking this walk down memory lane?"

Pierre shrugged easily. "Me, I am thinking how the war is behind us and yet the danger is with us still."

"You don't seem very troubled by the thought."

"Ever since the Bible lesson with M'sieur Levy, I have been thinking," Pierre said. "My life is good these past weeks. Very good. I am married to a wonderful woman. I have work that could be worthwhile if only the politicians would let me get on with it. My country is at peace once more. And I have friends. Good friends."

"Thanks," Jake said. "And likewise."

"And," Pierre continued determinedly, "I am thinking that I have begun to let my faith slip. I realized that last night. I have started to take my prayers and my studies more lightly. I do not seek to learn so swiftly now, because life is good." Pierre glanced toward him, somber now. "But life moves in circles, does it not? Just as with politics and diplomacy and the currents of conflict that surround us."

"Just who," Jake asked quietly, "is the teacher, and who the student?"

"It is my responsibility to use these good times to prepare for the bad," Pierre went on. "It is an opportunity I cannot afford to pass up. I can only remain strong and steadfast if I see these quieter times as opportunities to grow."

"To prepare," Jake added, admiring him.

"The Bible teaches me that with my faith I am building my life upon a strong foundation," Pierre agreed. "But still it is *I* who must *build*."

They passed the village's outskirts, and gradually the congestive grip on their speed was loosened. Jake said with a smile, "'The Boogie Woogie Bugle Boy of Company B.' You remember that one?"

"The Andrews Sisters." Pierre laughed. "Oh yes. He made the company jump when he played reveille, blowing eight to the bar. I loved that song."

"And Benny Goodman," Jake recalled, grinning. "I remember when he came out with that new girl singer, Peggy—"

Then they were hit. And hit hard.

"Sir? Can you hear me in there?"

Jake stirred, groaned, shifted, and felt the glass around him tinkle and settle. He came fully alert, swung his head, felt a swooping panic when he saw that the driver's seat was empty. "Pierre!"

"Over here, my friend," he said through Jake's shattered window. "Can you move?"

Jake winced at the lance of pain caused by the nodding of his head. Pierre was bleeding from a gash in his forehead, but otherwise he seemed all right. "I think so."

"Easy, sir," Samuel Bailey said. "You took quite a hit."

Jake reached for the door handle, realized it was not where it was supposed to be. Gradually the idea worked through his fuzzy brain that neither was his seat. Jake struggled to orient himself and realized his entire side of the car had been shifted over a full foot, sitting now where the gearshift had formerly been, resting up alongside Pierre's seat. His side of the car was concave, and he was jammed in so tight his legs could not even move.

"You will have to slide up and out of my side," Pierre said.

Jake nodded, fought down a moment's panic when his feet did not respond to instructions, breathed more easily when he finally managed to extricate one leg.

Sergeant Adams stuck his buzz-cut and shoulders through what remained of Pierre's door and said, "Here, sir, let me help."

Limply Jake allowed himself to be gripped and tugged and pulled free. He half scrambled, half slid across and out of the door, then had to be helped to stand upright. He looked over to Pierre. "Are you all right?"

"It was your side that took the hit," Pierre pointed out.

Jake examined his friend. "Then why are you holding your ribs?"

"Colonel Burnes!" A familiar voice with its coldly polished tones called out. "I thank the heavens you are all right!"

"Back off," snarled a furious Sergeant Adams.

"Get out of my way, you oaf." An immaculate Dimitri Kolonov tried futilely to brush by the leatherneck. "Call off your dogs, Colonel, I beseech you."

But Adams was having none of it. He blocked the Russian's advance, then rounded on a second man, a heavyset fellow with the slanted features of a Mongolian. "Either of you try to take another step, and I'll make me a Russian sandwich."

"Really, Colonel, I must protest. This really does go beyond the bounds of decency."

Jake did his best to ignore the Russian, looked around, saw that their car had been pushed to one side of the road. The traffic roared by, unimpressed with just another roadside tangle of metal and broken glass. "What happened?"

"You got blindsided, sir." Samuel Bailey did not try to keep his words from traveling over to where the Russians stood. "We had these two in our sights, stayed between them and you the whole way, but just after we got through the village, this truck appeared out of nowhere and did its best to take you out."

Jake examined the wreckage, saw how his side had been bent to an almost horseshoe shape, gave silent thanks for the gift of coming out alive. "Where's the truck?"

"It backed out and took off," Bailey said.

"Not before the driver waved over at your little friend here," Adams added.

"This is preposterous," Kolonov snapped. "Such wild accusations are beneath men of our stature, Colonel."

Jake ignored the Russian. "Can we take your car?"

"We could have," Adams rapped out, remaining a one-man barrier against Kolonov's advance. "But our Russkie friends here managed to plow us into a wall."

"Outrageous. Colonel, I must protest. We were simply trying to avoid striking your unfortunate vehicle."

"You can go sell that one to the navy," Adams snarled, and shoved the burly guard hard when he took another step toward the group. "Back off, I said!"

"And now you resort to violence. Tch, tch, what a pity it had to come to this." Dimitri Kolonov gave a regretful smile and motioned toward a gap in the wall. Instantly two additional men appeared. "I regret to inform you, Colonel, that your man has provoked an international incident. These men are empowered by the Turkish Security Force and are here to place you all under arrest."

"They are as Russian as you are," Jake said.

"Acting as instructors to the local police, all official and aboveboard, I assure you." Dimitri showed a smooth palm. "I do hope you intend to come along without causing further embarrassment, Colonel."

"We've been set up," Adams snarled, trying to cover three directions at once.

"I thought there were more than two of them in that car," Bailey muttered.

"We are protected by diplomatic immunity," Pierre protested.

"Naturally, this must be checked out thoroughly," Kolonov purred as the two guards, joined by Kolonov's burly companion, began a flanking action. "But until such time as your consulates can confirm your official status, I fear that you must be treated as common criminals."

"It won't work," Jake said.

"Ah, but, Colonel, this is why your country fails so miserably at the great game. A delay here, another postponement there, and suddenly a new policy appears, making all your efforts futile."

Jake played for time, willing strength back into his legs, knowing he was not up to this. Not yet. He sensed more than saw both Bailey and Pierre begin sidling away from the confines of wall and car. "What is it that is so important about Kumdare?"

Kolonov gave the smile of a hungry cat. "A pity you shall never have the chance to find out, Colonel. I must warn you, my men are armed and prepared—"

A squeal of rubber, the blare of a horn, and a familiar voice shrieked, "*Jake!*"

"Now!" shouted Pierre, already airborne and spinning before the single word was out, slamming into one guard before the man had time to recover and go for his weapon. Adams and Bailey moved like a well-trained team, making short order of the other two. In the space of two breaths, the roadside was littered with three crumpled forms.

Pierre bounded to the waiting Citroen, pulled open the door, called back to Jake, "Anytime will do, my friend."

Jake refused either to limp or to wince. He moved stiffly but steadily for the car.

"I formally protest," Kolonov started. "This is a most—"

Jake looked through the open window as the Citroen rolled away and said, "Why don't you just blow it out the old kazoo."

"We are not out of the thicket, I fear," Phyllis declared above the sound of wind and roaring engine and squealing tires and a chorus of protesting horns. "Not yet."

"Their car wasn't in much better shape than ours, ma'am," Samuel Bailey pointed out.

"Unfortunately, most of their vehicles carry portable short-wave radios," Phyllis replied.

Pierre continued to look from Phyllis to Jasmyn and back as though to say, Look, see, this is how a woman should drive. "It is doubtful that a portable voice set would be able to reach Istanbul."

"They are highly amplified," Phyllis replied. "The most modern available."

Jake slid down another notch, so that the wildly swinging scene in front was more fully blocked by Bailey's shoulders. "How do you know all this?"

"I told you about the Circle of Friends," Sally said. She was wedged so tightly into the backseat that even

turning toward him was an effort. She asked for the
tenth time, "Are you sure you're all right?"

"Fine, just a little bruised."

"You look so pale."

Jake winced as the great black Citroen hurtled
around a slow-moving cart, into the flow of incoming
traffic and back again so fast it was hard to believe it
actually happened. He held grimly to his thought
rather than give in to the rising terror. This woman was
worse than Pierre. "No amateur organization would
make it a practice of knowing the type of equipment
carried by Soviet spies."

"Speaking of amateurs," Pierre murmured from the
other side of the backseat, "my hat goes off to you, madame. I would be most grateful for the chance to take
driving lessons from you someday."

Corporal Bailey swung around to nod agreement in
Pierre's direction. "I gotta agree with you, Major. Up to
this point, I would have said you were the cat's meow.
But this dame, I mean, Mrs. Hollamby here, she's in a
class of her own."

"Nonsense," the old lady demurred, as a faint flush
of pleasure crept up her neck. "I have simply adapted
to the world in which I live."

The two Marines sat up front with Phyllis; Pierre
and Jake manned the two backseat windows with their
wives in between. Jasmyn had hardly breathed, much
less spoken, since the journey began. The one advantage to their cramped backseat was that it kept Jake
from bouncing about. Every inch of his frame seemed
to be bruised and complaining.

From his corner position, Jake watched Sergeant
Adams grimace and shut his eyes as they came within
a hairsbreadth of plunging over yet another cliffside

curve. It gave him a sliver of comfort to know the leatherneck found this journey as nerve-grinding as he did. "I still want to know—"

"You are quite right, Colonel," Phyllis calmly acknowledged. "It is both a relief and a pleasure to know that we have allies of such caliber. You see, my husband was more than simply the head of a British company's local subsidiary."

"A spy," Jake said, the pieces falling into place. "He worked for the British Secret Service."

A flicker of approval passed through the rearview mirror. "Just so. He was a remarkable man, my husband, and it was a pleasure to work alongside him. As his health deteriorated, he increasingly came to rely on me. His decline began at the onset of war, you see, and he felt it would be an absolute crime to let our side down. Then, within a ten-month period, I suffered the double loss of both my husband and my son. Despite all my prayers, the resulting void threatened to consume me. Thankfully, by then Whitehall knew of my own efforts and began to treat me as an agent in my own right. The pressure of supplying them with information helped enormously to see me through that critical period." Another glance in the mirror, this one directed toward Sally. "It was a true godsend, the fact of being not only needed, but actually important in such a crucial period."

Sally asked, "And the Circle of Friends?"

"All true," Phyllis replied. "And all amateurs. Which is one reason they have continued to remain such a valuable asset."

"And you are their conduit."

"Quite so, Colonel." Phyllis entered and departed from a village so fast that all they saw of it was dust and blur and a few scattered feathers. "And their filter. I fear the dear ladies in their unbridled enthusiasm pass on a great deal of chaff with the grain."

"I would be honored if you would call me Jake."

"Why, how very gallant. It would be an honor."

Pierre cleared his throat. "I still fail to see the need for concern over what the Russians will be able to pass back to Istanbul."

"As to the exact range of their radios," Phyllis said, "I am not certain. But I do know they would have been able to pass on the information through a more powerful channel."

"Of course," Sally cried. "The ships!"

Jake winced at the sudden pain of trying to swivel and look down at Sally. "What ships?"

"This way, hurry!" Despite the need for her cane, Phyllis set a pace down the boarding ramp that had them all trotting to keep up. The next departure was a passenger ferry, so she had blithely swung into a space far too small for her enormous vehicle, and led off on foot. She had timed their rush for the boat perfectly, for as the last of them scampered on board the ropes were cast, the whistle blown, then the ferry shuddered and started off. Jake leaned heavily against a metal pillar and searched the docks, but could see no sign of pursuit.

"Maybe she gave them the slip," Bailey offered hopefully.

"More likely," Pierre replied, moving up alongside, "they have decided to concentrate their forces closer to the lair."

"I fear the major is correct," Phyllis said.

Sally slipped her arm around Jake and asked yet again, "Are you sure you're all right?"

"How could he be? He has survived an attack from the Russians that clearly has rattled his bones." Phyllis pointed her cane toward a set of empty deck chairs. "Really, Colonel, I must insist that you sit down. Your day is far from finished."

Jake sighed his way over and down, as tired and battered as he had felt in his entire life. The group moved with him, settling into nearby benches, pulling over available chairs. "I do not see," Pierre said, "how you can be so sure this Kumdare site is truly intended as an observation post."

"Harry told me the same thing on the phone," Jake said. "Or tried to."

"It is the perfect location," Phyllis replied. For all her years, the day appeared to have left no mark on her at all. If anything, she seemed to have taken nourishment from the excitement. Her voice remained fresh, her eyes sparkling and alive. "This stretch of water is like the narrow neck of a bottle. Any ship wishing to enter the Mediterranean Sea from either the Caspian or the Black Sea has to pass through the Bosphorus."

"And those two seas," Pierre murmured, "are the locations of the Soviet Union's only warm-water ports. The only ones not shrouded in ice for several months a year."

"Precisely," Phyllis said approvingly. "Russia has sought to conquer Istanbul for centuries, back even when it still was known as Constantinople. Czar Ivan the Great went so far as to call it the key to world dominion. Capturing it would open the vast wealth of all southern Europe and northern Africa to direct attack.

Britain has gone to war with Russia over this narrow passage no fewer than four times. After the last battle, a pact was finally signed that permitted Russian vessels free passage through the strait, but only so long as they carried neither weapons nor munitions."

Jake struggled to cast aside the rising wave of fatigue and demanded, "Then why all this subterfuge about a cultural center? Why not simply open up a watch station and be done with it?"

"Two reasons. First, because Turkey stands at the edge of a political precipice. And second, because too many of our politicians stubbornly insist on seeing Russia as our gallant ally. They have too much invested in this friendship to accept that Stalin and his minions are as power mad as the worst of the old czars. What they fail to accept is that the Soviets are seeking to gain through subversion and deception what they could not obtain through force of arms."

"They are trying to install a Communist government here," Sally offered.

"Not only Communist," Phyllis said, casting her an approving glance. "They want a puppet regime under Moscow's direct control. Even as we speak, we are witnessing the same tragedy happening throughout all of Eastern Europe. That is why this station is so vital to all our interests."

Despite his best efforts, Jake found it impossible to keep his eyes open any longer. The lids fell as though louvered down, the voices mingled with the rumbling motor and the wind and the cry of gulls, and he was gone.

Chapter Fourteen

J ake?" Sally's gentle hand rocked his shoulder once more. "We're there."

He groaned his way to wakefulness, feeling he had been asleep for less than five minutes, then groaned a second time when his muscles complained stiffly. He let Pierre and Samuel Bailey help him to his feet because he had to. Phyllis watched sympathetically as he tried to unleash his complaining limbs with a few simple stretches. "If it is any consolation, Colonel, the fact that the Russians went to all this trouble is a clear indication that they consider you a grave threat to their plans."

"I guess I should be grateful," Jake said, wincing as the boat jammed the dock and knocked them about.

"Be glad you are alive," Pierre said, offering Jake his arm. "When that truck appeared from nowhere, I thought we were both leaving this earth for good."

"Don't talk like that," Jasmyn said sharply. "Not ever."

"Come," Phyllis said, starting for the lowered docking platform. "Those waiting taxis will soon be taken."

By the time they made it to the rank of antiquated vehicles, Jake's legs and his mind were moving a bit more comfortably. He said to the two Marines, "I want you to take a second cab."

"Good, a plan," Pierre said, his mobile features rising in a vast smile. "I find great relief in the news, my friend, that your head is working once more."

Jake ignored him. "They'll probably be watching the consulate entrances."

"Most certainly," Phyllis interjected.

"We'll take one taxi and work up a diversion. See if we can get them to follow us. Then you two scramble over the side wall and make like greased lightning for the consul general's office."

"You can count on us, sir," Bailey said.

"An excellent plan," Phyllis said. "I remain most impressed with you, Colonel."

"If for any reason Knowles isn't available, head for Barry Edders. Tell him we have concrete proof that the Russians are sabotaging the construction of our observation post in Kumdare. Inform him also of the reason behind it, this sighting of Soviet warships making way for the Bosphorous, and through that into the Mediterranean, in direct breech of international treaty."

"Consider it done," Sergeant Adams assured him.

Jake turned to Phyllis. "I can't thank you enough for everything, ma'am."

The old lady raised herself to full height. "And just what do you intend to do," she demanded imperiously, "once you have managed to draw attention your way?"

"Run," Jake said, turning back to the Marines. "Everything depends on you getting through."

"Like the corporal says," Adams replied, his chin as aggressive as a battleship's prow. "We won't let you down."

Jake nodded, turned to Sally. "I want you to go with Phyllis."

"There is absolutely no way I am letting you go off on your own, the state you're in," she said, her eyes flashing fire. "So you can just put it out of your tiny little mind."

"And you, don't even start," Jasmyn warned Pierre before he could even get out the first word.

"Quite right," Phyllis said crisply. "I shall not be brushed off so lightly either, young man."

Jake looked from one stubborn woman to the other. "Listen—"

"You're wasting valuable time, Jake," Sally snapped.

"Indeed so," Phyllis added primly. "And just where on earth did you intend to run?"

"Heads up, everybody," Jake said, as their taxi rounded the final corner and the consulate gates came into view. "Here we go."

Their vehicle had the single grace of being large; the ancient Packard had no doubt once been a proud touring car, but time and neglect and countless miles of bad roads had reduced it to a creaking, amiable wreck. The driver was as friendly and elderly as the car and as tiny as it was huge. He was almost lost behind the massive steering wheel. A change of gears meant lunging to one side and ducking his head beneath the dash, momentarily losing sight of their direction, so he drove almost entirely in second. Jake felt his hackles rise at the thought of trying to lose a pursuit in this rocking bucket of bolts.

The simple fact of being the only person who could communicate with the driver had granted Phyllis pride of place. She sat erect in the middle of the front seat, with Jasmyn beside her. Sally sat in the backseat between Jake and Pierre.

When the consulate came into view, Jake tensed at the sight of three cars and a dozen stern-faced men blocking their entry. A pair of Marine guards were arguing and gesticulating for the men to move their vehicles. They refused to budge.

Sally abruptly leaned across Jake and shouted through the open window, "Oh no, it's them! Quick, quick, let's get out of here!"

The angry arguing cut off as though a switch had been hit, and the men watched open-mouthed as the car ambled good-naturedly past their station. "Hurry, hurry, they'll see us!" Sally added for good measure. Then she leaned back and accepted the men's astonished gazes with a satisfied smile. "I think that probably lit a fire under them, don't you?"

Phyllis directed the driver down a narrow side street. He cackled delightedly and did as he was told. Jake shot a glance through the back window and caught sight of a Keystone Cops maneuver, a dozen men colliding with one another in a mad scramble for their cars. When an ancient building blocked them from view, he turned back and asked, "Any chance of going a little faster?"

"This appears to be the best he can manage," Phyllis said, pointing him down another lane more narrow than the last. "Besides, our best hope rests not in speed, but in subterfuge."

The old city's lanes were a maze of contradicting directions. Jake soon lost all track of where he was or where they were headed. Phyllis, however, did not waver for an instant. The driver followed her directions with affable chatter, clearly enjoying himself immensely.

They entered a small square and stopped before a cavernous opening. "This is it," Phyllis said. "Everyone out."

The driver clutched his pay in one hand and waved them away with a final cackle and a grin of dark-stained teeth. Jake eased the ache in his back and legs, asked, "Where are we?"

"The Grand Bazaar," Phyllis said, stumping ahead at a rapid pace. "And now I really must ask that we make haste."

Cool shade swiftly replaced the sun's blazing heat as they walked down the gently sloping avenue and entered the bazaar. Within the winding lanes, walking vendors sold sticky sweets from great wooden trays, while others advertised water and tea with creaking cries, dispensing their wares from huge copper urns carried on their shoulders. Shop displays spilled out into the lanes, colorful pageants of carpets or spices or bronze tables or gold jewelry, stacked far above Jake's height. Old men sat outside shops now run by a younger generation, playing backgammon on boards so battered the triangular patterns were mere shadows on the wood. Their fingers picked and tossed the dice and slapped the pieces with such rapidity that from a distance the games sounded like a continual drumroll. Occasionally a youngster would come and whisper in an elder's ear; replies and advice were granted without a moment's pause in the game.

"Under the Christian emperors, traders from Amalfi, Genova, Pisa, and Venice were all granted commercial rights on the boundary between Europe and Asia." Despite her rapid pace, Phyllis still found both breath and interest to tell them of their surroundings. "The Grand Bazaar is the largest commercial site of its kind in the world and was established and built for these traders, largely in the form you find it today. Just as then, its sixty streets are divided up among various crafts. There are more than four thousand shops, backed by small factories and countless warehouses. Come."

She led them into a tiny store selling bright multicolored cloth for drapery and upholstery. She stopped and shook hands with the stallholder, turning to introduce her gathering. The slender merchant bowed his welcome and made a gesture for them to be seated. Politely Phyllis spoke a few words, and instantly his demeanor changed. He gave a second bow, this one of hurried respect, then walked to the back of his little shop. He glanced to ensure that the front entrance remained empty, then swept back one broad Venetian cloth to reveal a small door. Jake ducked his head and followed the others through.

Behind was a narrow series of chambers, one after the other, each occupied by a hand-operated loom. The men worked in undershirts—not against the heat, for the rooms were almost chilly in the enclosed gloom, but rather against the closeness of the air. As Phyllis led the others unerringly down the constricted passage, the workers observed their progress without pausing in their work.

Phyllis stopped within an end chamber that obviously served as storeroom, empty and dark save for the light from the previous chamber. She pointed at a ring set within the floor. "I must ask the major to kindly assist me."

"Most certainly, madame," Pierre said, and bent to the task. The thick-planked door creaked and groaned and reluctantly opened. Jake peered through, saw only blackness.

Phyllis lifted a battered lantern from its nail and carefully lit it. "There is a compass in the base. Be careful that you do not spill fuel when you take it out, for this is your only light."

Sally peered into the gloom and asked, "What is it?"

"The reservoir. Take care. The steps have not been used in years."

Even Pierre showed doubt over the sheer blackness beneath them. Phyllis gestured impatiently. "You must hurry. A boat waits at the base of the stairs. And be most careful." She jammed the lantern into Jake's hand. "Go directly north. About a kilometer away there will be a series of slits making a circular pattern of illumination. It is an ancient water tower. There are stairs leading up to a street-level door. I will be waiting for you there with a car."

Jake fingered under the lantern, undid rusty catches, pulled out an ancient compass in a cracked leather case. "You're sending us down into the sewers?"

"Listen to what I am saying," she said impatiently. "This was the city's water supply, built by the Romans. It is vast. A hundred years ago, two British explorers set out by boat to find the other side. They were never heard from again." She gestured toward the black hole. "Remember, go directly north. Do not stray at all from the course."

Jake watched Pierre gingerly feel his way down, bent over, and handed his friend the lantern. In the ruddy glow he glimpsed a small concrete station with dark waters lapping on all sides. He helped Sally and Jasmyn down, then looked at Phyllis. "What about you?"

Despite the gloomy shadows, her smile showed clear. "Who on earth would dream of making trouble for a harmless old woman? Now go. I will meet you at the water tower."

Jake was greeted underground by a sleeping head.

The stone guardian had long since fallen over on its side, the face now resting half submerged. Even so, it was broader than Jake was tall. He stepped onto the nose, grasped the ear, and swung himself up and over the chin. He stood and saw that attached to the back was a small rowboat. "It's here."

"So are they," Pierre hissed. "I can hear them talking above us."

Sally hesitated and demanded, "What about Phyllis?"

"We won't do her any good in jail," Jasmyn pointed out.

"Or wherever else it is they plan to keep us," Jake agreed, and eased himself down by a series of pitted footholds. He helped Sally and Jasmyn down to Pierre's waiting arms, watched them settle in the stern, then stepped into the unstable boat and centered himself with one hand on each gunnel. Once in the bow, he accepted the lantern from Pierre and watched as his friend stripped off his shirt and draped it over the light. Instantly they were enveloped in impenetrable gloom.

Sally started, "What—"

Pierre hissed for silence just as the darkness was illuminated again, this time by a flashlight beam from above. Not trusting the oars to move silently, Pierre lifted one out of the oarlock and gingerly steered them away. Voices called back and forth, the noise echoing through vast distances. Jake craned, searched, saw no end or wall or marking. Just a forest of huge pillars rising from the black waters, stretching out in every direction as far as he could see.

Quietly Pierre paddled on one side, then the other, steering them from one great pillar to the next, placing ever more distance between them and the searching light.

"We might as well admit it," Pierre said, not bothering to whisper any longer, and uncovering the lantern to reveal worried faces.

Jake leaned back from his turn upon the oars, agreed wearily, "We've gone a lot farther than a kilometer."

"We are well and truly lost." Reluctantly Pierre turned to where voices bounced and echoed behind them.

"I guess you know what that means." Jake massaged his back with both hands, searched the great vaulted ceiling overhead.

"It is our only hope of ever finding our way out again," Pierre agreed resignedly. "Here, my friend, let me take up the oars again."

Carefully Jake traded places, then tried to give Sally a reassuring smile as Pierre steered them around and back toward the echoing voices. She did her best to reply in kind, despite the worried light to her eyes.

It had proved far harder than they had expected to maintain a steady northward course. The vast reservoir was actually split into a myriad of chambers by pillars that grew into long sweeping walls. Earthen embankments rose like shallow shorelines, looming suddenly upward to connect with the ceiling high overhead. Jake held his lantern up high, recalled Phyllis's warning about the two British explorers, and hoped desperately they would at least be caught in time.

Time passed in agonizing dips of Pierre's oars until a flashlight beam split the darkness and a great shout of triumph sounded from close at hand. Soon a pair of boats were winging toward them, hemming them in, as more shouts and calls bounded back and forth around them. They were swiftly ringed by boats. Turks rowed toward them, under the careful supervision of lighter-skinned silent men. A rope was tossed and made fast to their bow. They were all too tired and dejected to protest as they were rowed back in the direction from which they had fled.

Wearily Jake assisted the ladies up and back over the great leaning face. He ignored the proddings and shouted orders, and climbed up the rusting ladder into the little storeroom. It was almost without surprise that the first words of English he heard came with the polished accent of a victorious Dimitri Kolonov. "You have given us quite a mad chase, Colonel. A pity that it must now end with you and your associates occupying a pair of rather dank and musty cells."

"I think not," another voice said, startling them all.

Jake raised his exhausted head, squinted through the gloom, and saw Consul General Tom Knowles stride into the crowded room. He was flanked by a grim-faced contingent of Marines. Knowles marched straight up to the dumbfounded Russian and said, "I am formally taking charge of these people."

Phyllis Hollamby's gray head appeared behind Tom Knowles. She smiled at Sally and explained, "When you failed to arrive, I decided, as they say, to call out the Marines."

Sally beamed back in undisguised relief. "I'll find the words to thank you someday, I'm sure."

Dimitri Kolonov's mouth worked several times before he managed, "Really, I must protest. These people have violated numerous statutes and must be held—"

"In protective custody under my personal supervision," Knowles snapped back. "I remind you that they are all holders of diplomatic immunity."

The Russian's eyes scampered frantically for another ploy, but he could manage only, "I must warn you, my superiors will raise serious protest at this affair."

"On the contrary, it is *I* who must warn *you*," Knowles replied, his eyes hard as bullets, "that you are on the precipice of creating a major international incident."

Impatient at this palaver in a tongue he clearly could not understand, one of the Turkish police grabbed Jake's arm and roughly pulled him to his feet. Before he could protest, a shrill lash of Turkish froze the room. Anya Ecevit stepped from behind the consul general to unleash a full barrage upon the Turks. They stepped back, clearly cowed by the onslaught. Only when there was a circle cleared about the four did she pause, turn to Jake, and say, "Are you all right, Colonel?"

"Fine," he said quietly. His head felt ready to burst from the aching fatigue.

"You don't look fine," Anya said. "You look beyond exhausted."

"Enough of this malarkey." Knowles dismissed the Russian and his minions by simply turning his back on them. "Sergeant, you and your men help these people along."

"Right you are, sir." The sergeant glided over and offered Jake a supporting arm and a grin. "It'll be a pleasure."

Chapter Fifteen

Ah, Colonel, come in, come in." Tom Knowles was already on his feet as Jake pushed the door open. "Hope you're feeling better."

"Fine, sir." Two days' rest had restored Jake in both mind and body. Not to mention the lift he had just received when Anya Ecevit had greeted him with the news that Charles Fernwhistle had been recalled to Washington. Jake took the offered seat and nodded in reply to Barry Edders' broad smile. "Ready to get back to work."

"Glad to hear it. A great deal has been happening, and even more is left to do." Knowles nodded toward his political officer.

"Right." Edders made a futile gesture to straighten the folds of his rumpled suit. "As you have no doubt gathered, Europe finds itself facing more than simply the peril of war's aftermath."

"Soviet aggression," Jake offered.

"Exactly," Knowles agreed, too animated to release the topic to Edders' care. "One by one, the nations of Eastern Europe have begun falling like dominoes, entering into the nightmare of total Soviet Communist domination."

198 ❖ *Rendezvous With Destiny*

"There was a hurried conference in Washington the day before yesterday," Edders continued, "followed by an emergency meeting of both houses of Congress yesterday. Your findings were included in the President's address."

Jake sat up straighter. "What?"

"This is of the utmost importance," Knowles assured him. "President Truman has informed Congress that unless vital emergency aid is sent immediately to the prodemocratic governments of Greece and Turkey, within months they could both fall to the Soviets."

"Maybe even weeks," Edders added gravely. "We're talking right down to the wire here."

"In the face of this potential disaster," Knowles went on, "the President requested that a special aid package be offered to these nations, so long as they are willing to fight openly against Communist aggression."

"They're already calling it the Truman Doctrine," Edders said. "I saw it on the wire this morning."

"The aid you have been sent to handle is merely the first trickle of a growing flood," Knowles told him. "It is vital that two things happen, and happen immediately. First, that people such as yourself are chosen to handle the funds in a manner which remains totally removed from bureaucratic battles. And secondly, we must ensure that the disbursement of these funds fosters this country's democratic process and the growth of their private sector." Knowles eyed him gravely. "With your agreement I will offer my strongest recommendation that this task be kept in your most capable hands. It will be an enormous and largely thankless undertaking. But I could think of no one more suited to the challenge."

•   •   •

Jake glanced at his watch—a half hour yet before Sally was to join him for lunch. Sally and Jasmyn were like two excited children, full of plans to turn their vast apartment into a joint home. This ability of hers to go from sharing his work and his life to delighting in being a housewife amazed him.

Yet in his impatience to share the news of his appointment with her, time seemed to hang as still as the dust-laden heat. He looked out his window, where through the trees' leafy green towered ancient domes and minarets. Numerous mosques rose and fell like man-made hills.

Directly below him, the streets were a constant, tumultuous theater. Young men pushed great handcarts bearing everything from logs to spices to carpets to bronze. A boy walked by balancing a folded cloth on his head, upon which was balanced a broad metal platter; on the platter was a pile of soft pretzels as tall as the boy. Jake watched him saunter down the slippery cobblestone lane, calling out to each passerby and doorway, accepting coins and pulling out wares, all without losing his balance.

In the far distance, Jake could catch a glimpse of boats nestled up to ancient docks or resting gently at anchor in the protected waters of the Golden Horn. There was a stillness to the noonday air, a vibrant sense of timeless energy so magnificent it made mockery of all human noise and strife and ambitions.

Jake swung about at the sound of a quiet knock at his door. "Come in."

Daniel Levy entered. "I hope I am not disturbing you."

"Not at all. Have a seat." Jake unleashed his grin. "It looks like your job is going to be more permanent than either of us had dared hope."

"You are staying on, then." The bearded man sighed his relief. "That is wonderful." A nervous tug at his beard, then he added, "My father will be pleased as well. He has asked when you will be returning for another lesson."

"Tell him," Jake replied, "I'd like to make it a regular event, if it's all right with him."

Daniel hesitated, his eyes downcast, then said quietly, "There is another side to the book you saw, the *Me Am Lo'ez*. I did not discover it until our lives were disrupted by the war, when we were settled in the camp. But it was there all along." He raised his head, asked Jake, "Have you ever heard the word *pilpul*?"

Jake resisted the urge to steer the conversation forward, much as his mind wanted to return to the gladness that the day contained. There was something here, some opening that his mind did not recognize, yet was clear to his heart. He could sense an opportunity, a purpose to the moment. So even though his head and his world clamored to race on and leave the opportunity and the quietness behind, he settled back and said as calmly as he could muster, "I don't think so, no."

"It is a Yiddish word, and means a meandering argument with no real purpose or direction. Like many such expressions, it has a meaning that can only be understood through example." The dark gaze turned away and inward, not seeing the room and the brilliant sunlight filtering through the window. "I must speak again about our internment during the last stages of the war. Conditions inside the camp were not too bad. Oh, the food was awful, of course. The barracks were overcrowded and always either too hot or too cold. The camp itself was utterly bare."

"I could never imagine," Jake said quietly, "being falsely imprisoned behind barbed wire and then talking about it as calmly as you do."

"My people have learned to endure much," he replied, his eyes distant and sad. "But that is not what I wished to discuss. I mentioned it only for you to understand that it was not as the camps which you have seen. It was a camp, yes, and it was very difficult, but our greatest battles were against boredom and uncertainty. We did not know anything, you see, not what was going on outside the wire, nor what was to become of us. The soldiers themselves had been ordered to discuss neither with us. Any wisp of rumor swept through the camp like wildfire, and as usually is the case with such, almost all the rumors were bad. Worse than bad. Horrible. A mysterious truck with no markings was either delivering poison for our food, or cement to begin building the gas chambers. Dreadful rumors. In many respects, they were worse than the camp itself."

He lapsed into silence then, his face drawn, his expression brooding. Jake watched him for a moment, then granted him privacy by turning his attention to the street below his window. A pair of youngsters struggled by, one pushing and the other pulling at a spindly wooden cart piled with a mountain of turnips. The boys could not have been ten years old, yet they looked born to the task of toiling down the sweltering street, almost as ready to collapse as the overburdened cart. A very harsh land.

Daniel drew himself back with a sigh. "Where was I?"

"I'm not sure," Jake said slowly, turning back around. "You were going to describe for me the meaning of a word."

"*Pilpul*, yes, of course. Thank you. The imprisoned young men were truly beside themselves, as you can well imagine. Most were married. They only took those over eighteen years of age, you see, and it is our tradition to marry young. Many had families, babies, and no news. No word of how those families were keeping, where money and food were coming from, whether they too were perhaps being herded into camps."

Daniel shook his head slowly. "It was an awful time for many. They turned to talk of violence, some against the regime here in Turkey, which was ludicrous, of course, a paltry handful of Jews plotting the downfall of a regime governing a Muslim country of some fifty million. What did they expect, that suddenly the impossible would happen and a Jewish leader would be elected? But they were young, and they were frightened, and logic played little part in their discussions. The majority began making plans to emigrate. To leave their home of centuries and begin anew in Palestine. The thought of a free Israel gave many the focus they required, you see, to believe that there truly would be a tomorrow."

Daniel paused a moment, deep in memories, then continued, "A few of the elders gathered with the ones planning to emigrate. But most realized that they could not pull up the roots of centuries and move to a country that did not in truth exist. The uncertainty of such a journey was, at their age, beyond their ability to imagine. So they retreated into Torah.

"Night and day they gathered, little groups banded together around this vast camp, growing in numbers until some contained as many as a hundred or more graybeards. They would sit, and they would argue. Not discuss. Not debate. Argue.

"Did they offer answers to the young men who drifted listlessly about the camp? Did they lead them in prayers for their release? No. They sought escape into the minute. They argued over things of no value. Items so intricately complex that none but their inner circle could follow, much less care about."

He picked up a pen, studied it, set it down, all without realizing what he had done. "I will give you one example. In the first volume of *Me Am Lo'ez*, there is instruction given over the prayers that one should say before opening the holy Scriptures, and again when completing one's study. The reason for this is clear. Reciting these blessings shows that a person considers the holy words to be precious and that the act of study is an act of worship."

Daniel shook his head at the memory. "But the camp elders, they took this simple instruction, and they elaborated on it. They tore it apart with their endless questions and arguments."

"I think I see," Jake said, recalling another passage, one from the New Testament.

"They spent weeks arguing over points of no importance. If a person is up all the night and begins the day with a Torah reading, should he first say the morning prayers or the Torah blessing? If a person is reading the Torah and finds an error—remember, all our Torah scrolls are written down by hand—does he say the final blessing when he stops? Should he first take another scroll and repeat the segment as it is correctly written? If another scroll is opened, should the first prayer be repeated?"

Daniel tugged angrily at his beard. "On and on it went, with the arguments raging back and forth, day after day after day. At a time when unity among the Jewish community was most critical, these elders, these leaders of our people, would gather in groups and declare that other bands of elders were heretics. Worse than the nonbelievers, for they desecrated the name of Torah with their wild opinions. Such comments incited rages which shamed us all. And over what? Details which meant nothing to us, to our plight, to those among us who were racked with fear and worry and pain."

Daniel shook his head again bitterly. "That is why I have resisted returning to my studies of the Scriptures since we were freed from the camp. I cannot help but remember where such studies led us in our hour of greatest need."

When he was sure Daniel was finished, Jake said carefully, "There was another Jew who condemned the elders of His time for just such a waste."

Daniel looked at him, his focus slowly tightening. "This is Jesus, yes? You are speaking of the Christian *messach*?"

"I mean no offense," Jake said quietly. "But I thought I should at least tell you that He too spoke against the leaders who did not see to their people's dire needs."

Jake waited, knowing that to press would be to drive the moment away, possibly close the door for good. Either Daniel wished to hear or he did not, but it had to be his choice.

Daniel sensed the patience as an invitation, and the hand working his beard calmed to thoughtful stroking. After a long moment he said, as much to himself as to

Jake, "I have spoken to you of what has remained most troubling to my heart. You have listened as a friend. How could I do less?"

A friend. "Thank you," Jake said. "Can I read you something?"

"Of course." Daniel watched with widening eyes as Jake unbuttoned his shirt pocket and drew out his New Testament. "You carry your Bible with you?"

"I like to have it," Jake explained, hoping he could find the passage, "in case I have a free moment and want to stop and have a time of quiet."

"A time of quiet," Daniel repeated softly. "Such words from a man of such action."

"Here it is," Jake said. "Matthew 23:23. 'Woe unto you, scribes and Pharisees, hypocrites! For ye pay tithe of mint and anise and cumin, and have omitted the weightier matters of the law, justice, mercy, and faith; these ought ye to have done, and not to leave the other undone. Ye blind guides, which strain at a gnat, and swallow a camel!' "

Daniel eyed him gravely. "This Jesus of Nazareth said that?"

"He did indeed," Jake affirmed. "That and much, much more."